A perfe

"Okay, here's what I'm thinking." Larissa smiled slyly. "You start hanging out more with Toby, and then you drop in a few questions here and there. Nothing too obvious. Just real subtle stuff to see if he likes me."

"I don't know. . . ." I kept my voice neutral, but I was really feeling anything *but* neutral.

"It shouldn't be a problem getting info out of him," Larissa continued. "You guys get on great. He would definitely confide in you."

"Yeah, I guess," I replied.

"So what do you say?" Larissa poked me with the end of her Bic. "Perfect plan, huh?"

Right then I just wanted to pick up my books and run. Far away from study hall and far away from Larissa and Toby. But Larissa was my friend. And I had promised myself I would get over my crush on Toby. So now I had to prove it.

"Yeah, it's a perfect plan," I agreed.

Don't miss any of the books in SWEET VALLEY JUNIOR HIGH, an exciting series from Bantam Books!

#1 GET REAL
#2 ONE 2 MANY
#3 SOULMATES
#4 THE COOL CROWD
#5 BOY. FRIEND.
#6 LACEY'S CRUSH
#7 HOW TO RUIN A FRIENDSHIP
#8 CHEATING ON ANNA
#9 TOO POPULAR
#10 TWIN SWITCH
#11 GOT A PROBLEM?
#12 THIRD WHEEL
#13 THREE DAYS, TWO NIGHTS
#14 MY PERFECT GUY
#15 HANDS OFF!
#16 KEEPIN' IT REAL
#17 WHATEVER
#18 TRUE BLUE
#19 SHE LOVES ME . . . NOT
#20 WILD CHILD
#21 I'M SO OUTTA HERE
#22 WHAT YOU DON'T KNOW

What You Don't Know

Written by
Jamie Suzanne

Created by
FRANCINE PASCAL

BANTAM BOOKS
NEW YORK • TORONTO • LONDON • SYDNEY • AUCKLAND

RL 4, 008-012

WHAT YOU DON'T KNOW
A Bantam Book / October 2000

Sweet Valley Junior High is a trademark of Francine Pascal.
Conceived by Francine Pascal.
Cover photography by Michael Segal.

Produced by 17th Street Productions,
an Alloy Online, Inc. company.
33 West 17th Street
New York, NY 10011.

ISBN: 0-553-48724-8

Visit us on the Web! www.randomhouse.com/kids

Published simultaneously in the United States and Canada

Bantam Books is an imprint of Random House Children's Books, a division of Random House, Inc. BANTAM BOOKS and the rooster colophon are registered trademarks of Random House, Inc. Bantam Books, 1540 Broadway, New York, New York 10036.

PRINTED IN THE UNITED STATES OF AMERICA

OPM 0 9 8 7 6 5 4 3 2 1

To Spencer Montan

Anna

"You're not reaching deep enough!" Toby Martin boomed in a gravelly Mr. Dowd voice, holding up his hands in exaggerated frustration. "Show me the *fire* inside!"

"Shhh, guys," I hissed quietly as Larissa Harris erupted into a fit of giggles. We weren't exactly miles away from the theater where we'd been practicing for our upcoming Sweet Valley Junior High production of *West Side Story*. And I was worried that our director, Mr. Dowd, might hear Toby making fun of him.

Still, it was hard not to crack up as Toby launched into another Mr. Dowd impression.

"Speak from your gut!" Toby demanded, his mischievous brown eyes scrunched up in mock concentration.

Toby really is a great actor, perfect in the lead role as Tony for our production of the play. And besides being superamazing on the stage, he's also a very funny guy in person. And with his mop of curly brown hair, he's also *very* cute . . .

"I want passion, I want punch, I want performance! The three *ps*!" Larissa added, repeating Mr. Dowd's drama-club mantra. We all dissolved into laughter again as we rounded the corner of the hallway, safely out of range of the auditorium.

"I could use some of the three *ps* myself," Toby said, rubbing his stomach as we walked through the long, yellow-painted hallways of the school building. "Pizza, pizza, and more pizza. Acting really makes me hungry!"

"Didn't you already have pizza for lunch today?" Larissa asked as we rounded another corner. "Oh, wait, I forgot. Cafeteria pizza doesn't exactly qualify as pizza. You should come with us. We're headed to Vito's for a snack."

I nodded in agreement, sucking up the fresh air that was drifting in through the hallway windows. After all that recycled auditorium AC, it was a definite improvement. Bad air and bad food were the two worst things about being cooped up in school!

Toby pushed open one of the main doors, waited for Larissa and me to walk through, then followed us out onto the front steps and into the sunshine. A blue car was idling at the bottom of the steps, and a woman—I figured she must be Toby's mom—waved at us through the driver's-side window.

"Thanks for the offer, but I've got to run," Toby said. "I have a dentist appointment." He sighed, narrowing his eyes in disgust. "Tooth torture ahead! I guess the only *ps* I've got coming to me are a lecture on *plaque* buildup and the dangers of *periodontitis,*" he joked, flashing his perfect-toothed smile before heading over to the waiting car.

"Isn't he just a laugh?" Larissa linked her arm through mine as the car pulled away.

"Yeah, he's a laugh," I answered, smiling as I tried out the phrase.

I still can't help grinning at some of Larissa's expressions. Larissa is the daughter of a British diplomat, and she has this way-cool accent and a seemingly endless collection of words like *jolly* and *blooming* that make her seem so exotic. She's also a ninth-grader *and* has a tiny diamond nose stud that her parents actually *allowed* her to get. So she's not exactly lacking in the sophistication department.

"Toby is sooo great, don't you think?" Larissa murmured, a faraway look in her eyes. "Don't you think?" she repeated.

"Yeah," I answered, trying to keep my voice casual. "He's really cute."

I tried to smile, but inside my heart was flipping and flopping like a fish caught in a bucket.

Anna

Larissa and I had already had this conversation—a million times. She'd already told me how *great* Toby was, how *cute* he was, how *adorable* he was.

The thing was, I agreed. In fact, I felt the same way. That was the problem. I was stuck in what my father calls a "pickle." I'd liked Toby for almost as long as Larissa had. It had begun shortly after we all started hanging out together at drama club. I wished I didn't like him, and I'd been trying my hardest *not* to for Larissa's sake, but I couldn't help it.

For the longest time I wasn't sure if I really liked Toby in that way—I told myself that I liked him but I didn't *like* like him. Then when I realized Larissa liked him, I told myself I *couldn't* like him except as a friend. But I could never quite shake my feelings. Which meant now I had to hide them from Larissa because liking the same guy your friend does isn't exactly the way to *stay* friends.

Pretty complicated.

"I think he has a crush on me too," Larissa said excitedly, breaking through my chain of thought as we walked down the steps. She squeezed my arm, her green eyes twinkling brighter than her diamond stud. "I mean, I have a *feeling* he does. I don't have any proof. But sometimes you can just tell. . . ."

"I'm sure he does," I answered, trying to sound light and breezy and encouraging. "He totally likes you," I continued.

I didn't have to fake anything in my voice because I believed my own words. Of course Toby liked Larissa. He had to. *What's not to like?* I thought as we walked along the sidewalk. Larissa is classy and funny and a little bit wacky with her witchy-black eyeliner and killer sense of style. Besides, she and Toby were always kidding around together. *They're made for each other,* I thought sadly—and then immediately felt a flood of guilt for not feeling happy for the two of them.

Even just *thinking* about my disappointment felt like a betrayal of Larissa. I didn't think she had noticed anything funny about the way I was acting, but that didn't stop me from feeling like I had done something terrible.

After all, I know how it feels to be betrayed. Like when my two closest friends in the world, Salvador del Valle and Elizabeth Wakefield, liked each other and I found out the hard way—by hearing it from someone else. And the thing is, Salvador was supposed to be going out with *me*. Having your friend like the same guy you do and having him like her—and then finding out about it—is the worst feeling in the world! I'd *never* want to put anyone through that.

Especially not someone as cool and nice as Larissa, someone who had done absolutely nothing to me. Except be a good friend.

So just get over it! I told myself, stealing a glance at Larissa. She seemed to be off in her own happy little world. *What other choice do you have, Anna?*

I had to be firm with myself, and I had to start now. Because judging from the way things were going, it was only a matter of time before Toby and Larissa would be boyfriend and girlfriend. *And you wouldn't want to let them know how you feel and risk ending up with both of them mad at you.*

More than anything, I didn't want to lose any friends. Just the *thought* of losing someone makes my stomach go into a double sailor's knot. Ever since my brother, Tim, died, I've had this fear of losing people, and I guess I just want to cling to everyone I've got.

"Anybody home?" Larissa scrutinized me with a grin. "You look like you're miles away." I guess I was the one who was off in my own little world, not her.

"Uh, just thinking about all the math homework I've got," I lied, secretly amazed at how Larissa picks up on things so easily. It was yet another reason to protect our friendship—how many people are that sensitive and know their friends so well?

"Lighten up," Larissa added, pulling at my ponytail. "You take everything so seriously. You're what my mum would call a worrywart."

I tried to smile, but deep down I felt lower than a worm. Or a wart. And I wished I could be more like Larissa—carefree and fun and full of positive energy. The kind of girl Toby would go for.

But you're not, I corrected myself. *So just be happy for them instead of sorry for yourself!* Yep, no question: Toby and Larissa were a match made in heaven.

There was only one thing left to do: Get over this crush and move on with my life.

And I had to do it fast! Because it was starting to get hard to think about anything else.

Kristin

"Kristin, as usual you've done a great job with the calendar," Ms. Kern said as I finished reading out the monthly to-do list at our student-government meeting. "You're so organized! With a student president like you running this ship, who needs me?" she added.

I blushed with all the praise, and even though my face was as red as the beet salad my mom had packed for my lunch, I can't say I didn't appreciate it. Being the student-body president is really hard, and Ms. Kern's encouragement always helped me keep a positive attitude about the whole thing.

"Really, I'm very pleased with the way the student government is handling things," Ms. Kern continued, smiling at Bethel McCoy and the other representatives of the student body. "I'm not kidding when I say you guys don't need me," she added, and then coughed a little. "Which brings me to some news I'd like to announce."

News? I straightened up in my chair, feeling a

little tweak of worry skitter up the back of my neck. Now that I looked closely at Ms. Kern, her smile seemed a little bit forced. But maybe it was just my imagination. Maybe she was about to announce something really cool. Like a sudden increase in our annual student-government party budget. Or maybe she'd managed to convince the school faculty that we *really* needed to replace the Brady Bunch–era yellow-and-pink couch in the library.

"I'm afraid it isn't very good news," Ms. Kern continued with a sigh. My heart sank. I hoped it was nothing too serious, but another close look at Ms. Kern's face told me I was kidding myself.

"There's been a sudden illness in my family," Ms. Kern said in a low voice. "And I'm going to have to leave the school."

Leave the school? I blinked, shocked, as Ms. Kern went on to explain that she would be gone indefinitely. Maybe even for good. "We just don't know at this point," she said in a sad voice. "But my mother really needs my help, and so I'll be leaving for Kentucky next week."

Next week! I stared at Ms. Kern, my eyes as wide as saucers. Everyone else in the room was murmuring how sorry they were. But I couldn't say anything. The news was still sinking in, and I really didn't want to believe it. *Kentucky?* That was so far away from Sweet Valley it might as well be Siberia!

"The good news is that my replacement, Ms. McGuire, is one of my closest friends. So I feel confident that you'll all like her very much."

That was hardly good news. There was no way anyone could replace Ms. Kern as far as I was concerned. The thing is, Ms. Kern was more than just a regular teacher to me. She'd really been there for me from the very beginning, encouraging and supporting me even when I felt my very lowest. Like when Bethel was still mad at me for winning the election and would argue against all of my ideas. Ms. Kern helped me to handle the situation by pointing out that Bethel just needed to feel like her opinions still mattered. Once I understood that, I made a point of asking Bethel what she thought whenever possible, and we've been getting along much better ever since.

But it wasn't just school and student-government stuff that Ms. Kern had helped me with. It was everything. She'd always been so easy to talk to, and she'd always understood me. Unlike my mom, who's sometimes so concerned about my weight that she seems more interested in what I look like on the outside than what's going on in the inside.

"I'm really sorry to leave you in the lurch," Ms. Kern continued with a heavy sigh. "But I guess sometimes these things just happen."

She smiled bravely, but I could see tears glinting in her eyes. Poor Ms. Kern. She looked totally worn out, like all the sparkle had been sucked out of her.

"I hope your mom gets better soon," Bethel said as she and the others swarmed around Ms. Kern.

Me too, I wanted to add, but somehow the words just wouldn't come out of my mouth. All I could do was sit in my chair as numb and dumb as a block of wood, registering the horrible news. My ultimate favorite teacher in the world, gone, *maybe for good!*

I glanced down at the monthly calendar and looked through all the things we had to organize. *Wow.* And that was only for *one month.*

As we filed out of the room, I heard Ms. Kern call after me. "Kristin, could you stay behind a moment?"

I turned around reluctantly. Part of me had been hoping she'd single me out after the meeting, and part of me had hoped I'd escape without having to talk to her. I shuffled up to her desk, trying to think of the right thing to say. Obviously I wanted to wish Ms. Kern all the best. But somehow, even though I opened my mouth several times, nothing came out, and I just felt awkward and nervous. Luckily she started to talk first.

"I'm really going to miss everyone," said Ms. Kern, looking around the empty room with a trembling smile. "Especially you, Kristin." She always made me feel so special. "I hope to come back, but I'm just not sure when that will happen."

As Ms. Kern talked, I became more and more aware of my silence. And I was sure she was noticing it too. It's not like me to be quiet, *especially* around Ms. Kern. But no matter how much I wanted to say the right thing, I just didn't know *how* to say it. Everything I thought up sounded shallow and impersonal. I wanted to tell her I was sorry for what she was going through, but at the same time I couldn't help feeling sorry for myself. How could Ms. Kern just drop a bomb like this and expect me to handle it?

"You'll be fine without me," Ms. Kern murmured sympathetically as I looked down at the table, unable to meet her eyes.

Great, I thought miserably. Obviously Ms. Kern knew what I was thinking, and it made me feel horrible and embarrassed. Now *she* was trying to make *me* feel better when it should be the other way around!

I knew I was being selfish, but I just couldn't tell Ms. Kern that everything was okay and not to worry about me. Everything was *not* okay. Class president was a tough enough job with Ms. Kern around to help—how on earth was I supposed to manage without her?

"Kristin, you're awfully quiet," she said softly, her dark eyebrows furrowing with concern. "Do you want to talk about it?"

"No," I blurted out, my voice sounding much harsher than I meant it to. "No, it's fine," I continued weakly, grabbing my books and stumbling to my feet. "I'm sorry about your mother," I muttered, keeping my eyes on the floor, "but I'm late for English."

As I bolted from the classroom, a knot as hard and big as a peach pit formed in my stomach. I knew I'd let Ms. Kern down, and a part of me hated myself for it.

But another part of me felt as hard and heavy as the knot in my stomach. She'd let *me* down too. What would I do without her?

Notes Passed between Anna and Elizabeth during History on Monday

To Anna "The Clam" Wang,

So what's up w/you and Toby??? You haven't said a thing about him all day, which is so not like you. Is everything okay?

Curious Liz

Hey, Liz. Not much to tell. I guess I don't really like him all that much anymore. I think ~~Harriman's~~ Hairy Man's giving me the hairy eyeball, so I better pass this quick.

A–

What do you mean, you don't think you like him anymore? That was fast. Did something happen? You were acting a bit gloomy at lunch. . . .

–L

L–

Nothing happened. Toby's cool, but I guess I just like him as a friend. I was confused for a while, but now I'm sure I'm over it. Careful. Hairy M. is definitely on to us.

–A

Kristin

"Honey, Brian's on the phone," my mom called up to me as I lay on my bed, thinking about my awful day.

"Yeah, okay," I mumbled, sighing as I eyed the cordless phone on my nightstand.

Normally I'd have bolted across the bed and practically knocked myself out reaching for the phone, but at that moment I wasn't in the mood. Even for my boyfriend, Brian Rainey. Don't get me wrong—Brian is the best. But I just didn't feel like chatting.

As I reached for the phone, I considered asking my mom to tell Brian I was in the bathtub or something, but I knew if I did that, then she'd get all worried about me and want to talk. She means well, but she wouldn't get it. She'd probably just tell me I needed more exercise or to cut down on fats or something. *A good aerobics class is perfect for when you're feeling low!*

Yeah, right! I thought grimly. But if celery smoothies and Tae-Bo could help me be a good president without Ms. Kern around, I would have signed up right then and there.

"Hey, Brian," I said in my chirpiest voice, leaning back against my biggest, fluffiest feather pillow. "What's up?"

"What's wrong? You sound kind of flat."

That's Brian—it doesn't matter how hard I try to hide things; he can always sense when something's wrong. He just has this weird kind of radar thing when it comes to how I feel. Which is great—except when I don't feel like talking about it.

But soon enough I found myself blurting out the whole story—about how Ms. Kern was leaving, how lame I'd acted in front of her, and all my worries about being a good president without her. "She's just been so helpful," I explained. "And she makes student government fun. She's almost more like a friend than a teacher."

"It'll still be fun, Kris," Brian replied in his typically be-positive-and-it-will-all-work-out voice. "I mean, c'mon, you have all these people who look up to you and who are willing to help you. I, for one, will do anything you say. Just give me an order, Captain."

"I wish it were that easy," I said, chewing on a blond chin-length curl. "But you have no idea how hard it is. . . ."

Nobody did. Everyone thought being president was just about handing out questionnaires about the cafeteria food or deciding whether the queen of junior prom should have a rhinestone tiara or a funkier glitter headband. In my dreams!

In reality, there's way more responsibility involved. If I'd known that before I got voted in, maybe I'd have thought twice about being class president. But now it was too late, and I had a job to do. *Alone,* I reminded myself gloomily, feeling that peach pit in my stomach swell into something the size of a baseball.

"And it's not like you'll be alone," Brian tried to reassure me, as if he had read my mind. "Someone will replace Ms. Kern."

"Nobody can replace her," I blurted out, my voice all jangly with nerves. Yes, of course there would be a new adviser to help me run the student government—Ms. Kern had already told us that. But there was no such thing as a replacement for Ms. Kern.

"She's one in a million," I told Brian, examining the chewed lock of hair, which looked as miserable and pathetic and, well, *chewed up* as I felt inside. "I need *Ms. Kern's* guidance," I finished glumly. "And I guess that's history now."

"Well, there is someone else you can rely on for help," Brian suggested as I stared up at the ceiling of my bedroom, focusing on a tiny insect cocoon trapped in a spider's web.

Know how you feel, buddy, I messaged silently to the trapped insect, sighing. "And who's that?" I asked Brian. "Bethel? Because she's really busy too, you know, and I can't expect—"

"No, silly, *you!*" Brian interrupted.

"Huh?" Either I was being way dense or else Brian was, but something in this conversation just wasn't getting through.

"Kristin, you're missing the obvious," Brian carried on. "You're so busy thinking about how great Ms. Kern is that you're forgetting there's another really capable, really responsible person you can count on to run things—*yourself.*"

Then we're really in trouble! I thought with another sigh. Brian was being so sweet and supportive, but the flattery wasn't helping. Because when it came down to it, I just didn't feel that confident. Not without Ms. Kern.

"Look at you—you're organized, together, and motivated. . . ." I cracked a smile as Brian proceeded to tell me that I was far and away the best, most responsible school president SVJH had ever had.

"I also just happen to be your girlfriend, so maybe you're just a teensy bit biased," I said, laughing. Still, Brian's talk was starting to work.

At least I could actually laugh, even if my insides felt like they were stapled together.

"I mean, who could be a better president than you?" Brian said firmly. "You're smart, you're nice, everybody likes you. . . ."

"Keep talking," I said, another smile threatening to spread from the corners of my mouth. I didn't necessarily believe the stuff Brian was saying, but whatever! This pep talk was cheering me up.

"Seriously, what are you so worried about?" Brian insisted. "Ms. Kern has faith in you. Everyone does. You just need to have more faith in yourself."

"Okay, I'll try," I promised Brian, smiling. We talked for a few more minutes about other stuff going on at school, then hung up.

I lay back against my pillow. Maybe what Brian was saying wasn't so off the mark. After all, I had to have *something* good about me to get such a perfect boyfriend.

Though maybe perfect *isn't quite the right word,* I thought, shaking my head as I pictured Brian at home. No doubt he was wearing his trusty faded sweats and Stone Age skateboarding shoes with holes in the soles. *Now, if we could just fix that wardrobe . . .*

Anna

"Yo quiero, tú quieres, él/ella . . . ?" I grilled Larissa as we hunched over her books in the back of study hall. I had recently started tutoring her, and we were working on her Spanish homework. Quite unsuccessfully, I might add. We were both a little distracted—Toby just happened to be sitting a few tables ahead of us.

"Speaking of *yo quiero*—you know, what 'I want' and all of that," Larissa broke in with a mischievous whisper, "I really, really *quiero* some info on Toby. . . ."

"Larissa!" I sighed, trying to shush her by shrugging toward Toby, who was probably within earshot.

"Oh, don't worry about him—he can't hear us," Larissa said, grinning.

"Well, anyway, we should make the most of study hall and actually get some studying done. If you don't focus, you won't ace next week's quiz, and if—"

"I know, I know," Larissa interrupted me,

waving her hand. "If I don't ace the quiz, I'll get in trouble with my grades. And if my GPA drops to below a C, I'll be pulled from the play. But we both know that will never happen now that you're my tutor. . . ."

Larissa sure knew how to make things difficult. "Never say never," I said sternly, but I could tell she wasn't intimidated. "Now, you still need help in Spanish, so let's continue. Where were we?" I scrolled through Larissa's verb list, trying to at least *appear* focused but inside feeling every bit as twitchy and antsy as Larissa was.

I was still uncomfortable with this whole situation. It just seemed like such bad luck to be in the position of liking the same guy Larissa did.

But you don't *like him,* I reminded myself sternly as Larissa halfheartedly recited words from her vocab list. *Except as a friend.*

"*Un amigo, una amiga* . . . hmmm . . ." Larissa grinned and stared down at her Spanish book, looking interested for the first time in an hour. "Is *amigo* the word for *boyfriend* or just *friend?*"

"*Friend.* I think. Or maybe it means both. Like, depending on how it's used or something," I replied, flustered. Suddenly everything, even Spanish itself, seemed out to get me.

"That's confusing." Larissa frowned and snapped her gum.

Tell me about it! I swallowed and flipped through her dictionary, hoping to find words that had nothing to do with anything important. "Okay, Larissa, what's the word for *ankle?*" I demanded, feeling desperate.

Like *ankle* would be on the test! But it was worth a try. And at least *ankle* didn't have any double meanings, as far as I could tell.

"*Ankle* . . . Hello? Yoo-hoo!" I waved the book in front of Larissa as she stared off into space. "*Ankle—tobillo!*"

"I'm sorry, Anna." Larissa blinked her black lashes and shrugged apologetically. "I just can't concentrate on *anything* right now. Not until I know if Toby likes me," she added in an urgent whisper.

"But he does like you," I said, hoping that would be enough for her. It wasn't.

"I mean like me enough to be my boyfriend." She wasn't going to let go of it, was she?

"I'm sure he does. He's probably just taking his time and playing it cool." I hoped that would satisfy her.

Unfortunately it didn't. "But I *really* want to be a couple by opening night of the play. It's going to be really difficult for me to step aside when the kids with big parts get all the attention. But if I'm with Toby, I don't think I'll mind as much."

I couldn't blame Larissa for feeling that way.

She's so talented, and she had desperately wanted to be cast in a bigger part in the play. I could see how being with Toby would make a nice consolation prize.

I fiddled nervously with a button on my new pale pink sweater and noticed a long, loose thread—which I began to tug at instead of the button. I had to stay cool, calm, and collected over this whole Toby situation. My friendship with Larissa depended on it. Maybe even my friendship with Toby too, which used to be pretty good—until recently. Since I'd started thinking that I liked him, I felt tongue-tied and nervous around him. I wished I could just turn back the clock to when everything seemed simple.

"I'm *sure* Toby likes you," I murmured quietly to Larissa. "I'm also sure he wouldn't want you to fail Spanish!"

"Which is why *you* have to help me," Larissa hissed. "Anna, you and Toby are good friends. . . . Maybe if you spent more time with him, he'd open up. . . ."

"Open up?" I wasn't catching Larissa's drift.

"Okay, here's what I'm thinking." Larissa smiled slyly. "You start hanging out more with Toby, and then you drop in a few questions here and there. Nothing too obvious. Just real subtle stuff to see if he likes me."

"I don't know. . . ." I kept my voice neutral, but I was really feeling anything *but* neutral. Larissa's suggestion would be fine if I was just a regular friend and Toby was just any old guy. But he wasn't.

"It shouldn't be a problem getting info out of him," Larissa continued, excited about her plan. "You guys get on great. He would definitely confide in you."

"Yeah, I guess," I replied. I tried to look on the bright side: At least I *sounded* cool and unfazed, even though my entire body felt numb with dread. Larissa's words echoed in my head. Hanging more with Toby. That was the *last* thing I needed to do right now. If I was going to get over this crush, I had to *avoid* Toby, not hang out with him. It would be torture!

"So what do you say?" Larissa poked me with the end of her Bic. "Perfect plan, huh?"

Right then I just wanted to pick up my books and run. Far away from study hall and far away from Larissa and Toby. Everything about this setup was making me feel nauseated. It was totally reminding me of Elizabeth and Salvador and that whole confused triangle. They'd gone behind my back, and it had really hurt. And sometimes it still hurts to think that Elizabeth put her feelings for Salvador ahead of her friendship for me. Not to mention Salvador, who's been my absolute best friend since, like, the beginning of time!

I would *never* do that to someone. Which was exactly why I had to help Larissa. I just had to see things for what they were and stop making everything more complicated: She was my friend. And she liked my other friend. That was all there was to it.

Plus I had promised myself I would get over this crush. So now I had to prove it.

"Yeah, it's a perfect plan," I agreed.

And it would be. Things would work out fine, I told myself, smiling brightly at Larissa, but my heart was clanging like a gong. I yanked at the string on my sweater again. My outfit, my attitude . . . right about now, both seemed in danger of unraveling.

Toby

Tiene que sacarse esta muela. "This tooth must come out."

That was about the extent of my Spanish. Could you blame me? It was kind of hard to study with the whispery, giggly girls sitting behind me.

Tiene que sacarse esta muela. I stared dismally at the sentence I'd written down. I'd gotten my dentist, Dr. Gonzales, who's from Puerto Rico, to help me with my Spanish while he massacred my mouth yesterday. I guess that's what you get when you ask a dentist for help with your homework—a sentence about tooth decay.

Who knows, though. Sometimes our Spanish teacher, Señor Enrico, gives us weird topics to write on in his quizzes. And maybe, if I was lucky, this visit to the *dentista* would end up being worth the pain (literally!).

I sure hoped so because between my throbbing *muelas* and the noise emanating from Larissa and Anna's corner, I wasn't digesting any new vocabulary.

Toby

"Shhh!" I heard Anna hissing as Larissa stifled yet another loud giggle. I corkscrewed my head around to see what the fuss was about, but just like five minutes ago, the moment I looked at them, they looked down. Girls. I couldn't figure them out.

I'm not saying I don't like girls. Especially Larissa and Anna. I was really glad we all got to hang at drama. I mean, Larissa's always been a real blast to be around—she's extremely kooky and funny and loud, and I love that. I even used to have a bit of a crush on her.

But then I got to know Anna, and the crush on Larissa kind of faded into a just-good-friends kind of thing. Anna is so thoughtful and sensitive and really pretty, with jet black hair and skin that makes you think of a tall glass of milk.

Larissa is really cute too and has great style, but Anna is pretty in the way that makes me feel weirdly self-conscious, like you have something green growing out of your teeth or something. Once I started noticing how pretty Anna was, I definitely felt stranger around her. Nervous. But it was actually kind of exciting too . . . and it made my stomach do this out-of-control flip thing when I looked at her.

It was happening big time in study hall that day. I kept pulling these sudden head corkscrews and catching her eye before she looked down at her desk. Which made me feel . . . like I had something green growing out of my teeth! But the truth is, I really wasn't complaining!

Even the way she walked was elegant. Especially when she walked in my direction. Which she was doing right now.

"Hey, Toby, what's up!" Anna has two dimples that pop in when she smiles. Have I already mentioned that?

"Hey," I answered back. *Hey. Pretty clever . . .* not exactly the way to jump-start a conversation. Staring too much, saying too little. *Way to go, Toby!*

"What's going on?" Anna continued, pulling at a button on the cute pink sweater she had on.

"Nothing." Again the master of romance at work!

Still, she hadn't gone anywhere yet, so that had to mean something. And she came over to the front of study hall to talk to me specifically. Which also could mean something. I wasn't sure how to read the situation.

"Tooth okay? How are you feeling?" Anna asked with a kind smile.

"I feel like I'm drooling," I said. I meant because of my tooth, but I was afraid she might have misunderstood me. I certainly didn't want her to think I meant I was drooling over her. I tried to clarify myself. "I mean, you know how when you get work done on your teeth, your mouth can feel kind of, um, drooly afterwards?"

"Huh?" Anna looked confused. I swallowed nervously and ran a hand through my hair, cursing myself for being such a blockhead. I guess I was just so concerned about not having anything to say that when I opened my mouth, I just babbled randomly like an idiot!

"Sorry, I don't mean to gross you out. Anyway, they had to pull it out. So, *adiós*, molar!" I grinned, pleased to be making at least *one* joke.

Before all the crush stuff, it had been so easy with Anna. We would talk and laugh, no problem. But once I started *liking* liking her, everything I said seemed loaded and kind of awkward. Even she seemed to notice because she was much less chatty with me at rehearsal. Maybe because I was acting like an idiot!

"Did it hurt?" Anna furrowed her brow in concern. I have to say, it felt good to see the sympathy on her face. Maybe I could milk this tooth thing for all it was worth.

"Yeah, big time," I complained, rubbing at my swollen jaw. *"Me duele. Mucho!"* I grimaced even though it really didn't hurt *that* much. I guess I enjoyed the sympathy.

"Are you going to be able to sing at rehearsal?" Anna asked. "I mean, without hurting yourself more?"

Hmmm . . . opportunity to show her what a man I am. I pulled a long face and sighed. "It will hurt. But I can't let the cast down. I'll just have to get through it."

I sat back, waiting for the inevitable gush of sympathy for Toby the Brave. I felt a little guilty exaggerating my discomfort so much, but it was only because I liked Anna that I was doing it, so I figured it wasn't really such a bad thing to do. . . .

But just then the bell rang, and Anna flashed me an awkward smile. "Well—," she began. I was about to break in and ask her if she wanted to eat lunch with me and talk about the play, but Larissa called her name, and Anna suddenly spun around on her heel and darted back to get her books.

"Coming to lunch?" Brian Rainey asked me.

"I'll catch up with you in a minute," I said, looking around for Anna, who was now heading for the door and busily chatting with Larissa. I tried to hurry through the crowd of students shuffling out of the classroom to catch up with them, but they just disappeared into the hallway. And in a few seconds they were gone.

Toby

Weird, I thought. Anna had been chatting with me, and then she didn't even say good-bye.

But then again, she *had* been chatting with *me.*

It was all basically just very confusing. Like girls. Like girls and guys. Go figure. . . .

Kristin

"Kristin!" Ms. Kern looked genuinely pleased to see me and waved me into her office. "I was just cleaning out my desk. I'm glad you stopped by."

I smiled tentatively and walked into the office, trying to look together despite the fact that my legs were doing a Jell-O walk. I was ashamed of my behavior yesterday, and I knew I had to put things right between me and Ms. Kern. Part of me wanted to do a 180-degree turn and avoid such an uncomfortable conversation, but I knew I'd have to face up to myself if I did. And the truth is, I needed to say some things.

"I just thought I'd come and see how your packing was going," I said. I instinctively reached up to fiddle with a lock of hair—my trusty old nervous habit—but forced down my hand. I was an eighth-grader, not a kid. I was the student-government president. Ms. Kern expected more of me, and I needed to live up to those expectations. I owed her that at the very least after all the time she'd invested in me.

"Ms. Kern." I took a deep breath and made eye contact. Ms. Kern stopped what she was doing and smiled kindly, gesturing for me to sit. "I came to say that I'm really sorry for the way I acted yesterday. It was really immature."

There! I'd said it! Even just getting out those few words made me feel like I'd shrugged the weight of the world off my shoulders. A flood of relief filled my insides.

"I guess I was just being selfish," I explained. Ms. Kern nodded sympathetically—which just went to show why I liked her so much. I mean, she had every right to chew me out for acting so childishly, but instead she was just being understanding and patient. "It was wrong of me to be rude to you," I continued, keeping my voice steady. "But it's because I'm going to miss you so much that I acted the way I did."

"Forgiven," Ms. Kern said, her pretty face lighting up in a smile as she came over and gave me a hug. "I understand my leaving was a shock to you. It's a shock to me too." She pointed around her at the floor of her office, which was littered with stationery, potted plants, and piles of music books (Ms. Kern's also a music teacher here).

"As you can see, I'm completely unprepared for this! I mean, I thought I'd always be here. . . ."

She trailed off, her smile trembling, and I felt a rush of sympathy for her. She was obviously completely emotionally tapped out. Not to mention that she had to rush around, trying to pack. And all I'd been thinking about was myself.

"Here, let me help," I offered, dumping my book bag on a chair overflowing with papers and dropping to my knees to collect a pile of magazines that was threatening to spill over. "Do you have string?" I asked, feeling more and more at ease as I got into my busy-bee organizer mode. "And boxes? Because I know where we can get some boxes."

"Already taken care of," a strange voice broke in, and I turned to see a tall, skinny woman standing at the door, holding two large, empty packing boxes.

"Oh, I'm so glad you stopped by," Ms. Kern greeted the woman happily. "This is perfect timing. Joanne, meet Kristin Seltzer, our student-government president. Kristin, this is Ms. McGuire. She'll be taking over all of my classes, and she'll also be your new SG adviser."

Ms. McGuire flashed me a brief smile and nodded. She had very light, pale gray eyes behind horn-rimmed glasses and a supertight black bun with gray streaks.

"As I mentioned yesterday, Ms. McGuire is

also one of my closest friends," Ms. Kern continued, ushering Ms. McGuire into the small office. "So of course I feel extra confident that the two of you will get along great."

"I'm quite sure we will." Ms. McGuire smiled again. "So long as you're not afraid of good, hard work."

"Yes." I nodded. "I mean, no, I'm not."

I felt a little flustered. I guess it was just the way Ms. McGuire looked at me. Not unkindly or anything, but her eyes were kind of piercing, and everything about her was so immaculate and businesslike. It was sort of intimidating.

"So tell me about yourself, Kristin," Ms. McGuire said. She had a very sharp, flinty voice, unlike Ms. Kern, who speaks softly and with a lilty Southern accent.

"Kristin?"

"Oh, uh, sorry." I felt my face light up like a torch. I guess I was just so busy digesting the way Ms. McGuire looked and sounded that I'd kind of forgotten to answer her. "Myself. Um—well," I stuttered, scrabbling for words and drawing a total blank. It's hard to describe yourself, I think. Especially on the spot like that!

"Well, I'm, uh, I enjoy public speaking," I blathered, cringing as I realized that it had taken me, like, seven or eight pauses, *ums*, and *wells* to get a sentence out. Not exactly the mark of a good speaker, let alone a good public speaker.

"And how would you say others see you?" Ms. McGuire questioned. She was looking me up and down very carefully, her eyes seeming not to miss a thing.

It made me nervous.

"How do others see me," I repeated dumbly. "Well, I, uh . . . don't think about it very often, so it's, uh . . . difficult, I guess." I gulped weakly and tried to laugh. It came out more like a choke.

"She's very articulate, very organized, and confident!" Ms. Kern interrupted, smiling encouragingly at me. "Kristin is perfect president material. The students couldn't have chosen better."

Articulate . . . that's a stretch! I thought, groaning inside. I mean, this was the first conversation I'd had with my new adviser, and I was opening and closing my mouth like a guppy!

"So how are you enjoying your presidency?" Ms. McGuire regarded me intently as she settled into a chair and folded her hands in her lap, looking very serious. "Is it proving to be challenging?"

Not as challenging as this inquisition! I found myself thinking, though I felt a bit guilty for thinking it. After all, Ms. McGuire was probably only trying to get to know me a little since we'd be working together so much in the future. That was beginning to look like it might also turn out to be kind of a challenge. . . .

"It's hard work," I answered, lifting my chin and trying to look as confident as Ms. Kern was making me out to be. "But I think I'm up for it."

"I'm sure you are, Kirsten." Ms. McGuire smiled and adjusted her pearls.

"It's Kristin," I corrected as I took in how thin Ms. McGuire looked in Ms. Kern's chair. Another major difference between them. And I can't say it didn't add to my feeling of self-consciousness, seeing her long, thin legs and elegant, ballet-perfect arms. With Ms. Kern, I always felt more comfortable being plump because she's also curvy, but that kind of similarity definitely didn't exist between me and Ms. McGuire.

"Kristin. Of course," Ms. McGuire said brightly.

"Well, I'm very glad you two have met," Ms. Kern said happily, looking from me to Ms. McGuire. "It's good to know I'm leaving things in capable hands!"

"Of course you are," Ms. McGuire chimed in. "Kristin? What do you say we schedule a one-on-one as soon as I'm settled in?" She unsnapped a black patent-leather pocketbook and whipped out a matching day planner. "What day works for you?"

"Um, let me see." I scrabbled in my book bag,

looking for my schedule, but all I could see were piles of books and scraps of paper. *Organized.* Another word Ms. Kern could strike from the list of adjectives she'd used to describe me!

"Sorry, I can't find my schedule just now," I muttered, scrambling through all the junk. "I'm sure anytime would be fine."

"No problem. Just check in with me, and we'll schedule a time to liaise!" Ms. McGuire finished, unsnapping the lid of a silver pen.

Liaise? I nodded and walked out of Ms. Kern's office, feeling kind of wobbly and annoyed. I barely even knew what the word *liaise* meant, but I knew that it bugged me!

Ms. Kern! I'd been caught so off guard by Ms. McGuire and her fancy French expressions, I'd forgotten to say good-bye to Ms. Kern.

"Bye, Ms. Kern!" I stuck my head back in the classroom and waved at her, then started off down the hall. As I walked I thought about how, in a few days, I'd be saying good-bye to her for good. And then I'd be stuck with Ms. McGuire. How could my favorite teacher, someone I thought knew me so well, have thought I'd hit it off with Ms. McGuire? We couldn't be any more different. Ms. McGuire was more like the tiny patent-leather pocketbook she carried—which seemed to hold everything she needed just fine, and I was more like my supersize book bag—which was threatening to burst at the seams. I didn't think we'd gotten off to a good start.

"Hey, Kris!" Jessica Wakefield broke into my thoughts, smiling as she walked past with her twin, Elizabeth.

"Hey," I said, trying to sound cheery. A twinge of jealousy pinched through my insides as I watched Jessica and Elizabeth chattering away at the speed of light and looking totally carefree. The opposite of how I was feeling.

Or maybe I was just making too big a deal out of everything. Maybe Ms. McGuire and I would end up working totally harmoniously together, just like Ms. Kern said.

But somehow I doubted things would turn out as hunky-dory as Ms. Kern seemed to think. For one thing, Ms. McGuire's first impression of me couldn't have been too good.

And mine of her? Well, let's just say she was *nothing* like Ms. Kern!

Salvador

"So my brother offered to write me this video game that supposedly makes math fun," Blue explained to me, Anna, and Elizabeth as we sat at the lunch table. "I have to say, I'm pretty skeptical. I don't think anything could make me better at math."

"Why?" I grimaced as I bit into the cheeseburger I'd mistaken for a cheeseburger. Gristle and grease and something like cardboard for extra flavor does *not* make a real cheeseburger. I wanted to focus on the conversation, but the frightening taste sensation was getting in my way.

I forced myself to swallow the cheeseburger-like substance in my mouth and thought about Blue's words. It's not like I'm a geek or anything, but as I'd explained to Blue earlier, math *can* actually be fun. Once you get it. "It's not such a crazy idea, actually," I said. "I mean, math *is* like a game. You just need to figure out your strategies. Then you apply them and bingo—problem solved."

Salvador

"You are so lucky to have Leaf," Elizabeth said, picking at a fudge brownie. "Being raised by an older brother who's cool enough to make video games for a living—and still wants to help you with your homework. You should definitely take advantage of his offer."

"Tell me about it!" I agreed, trying to picture the Doña, my grandmother, who's raising me, putting together a video game for me.

"I still can't see it." Blue sighed, shrugging. "You can disguise sine and cosine as any action heroes you like, but when you get down to it, they're still math symbols, and they still confuse me."

"Well, sometimes life surprises you. I mean, look at my friendship with Anna," I said, breaking into a grin. "When I first met her, I thought she smelled really bad and I'd never want to be within ten yards of her, and now here we are, years later, best friends. Right, Anna?" I elbowed Anna, who'd been quiet and distracted all through lunch, absently toying with her so-called fettucini Alfredo (more like fettucini I'm-so-afraido). Anna's actually been my best friend since I can remember, and it's not unlike her to toy with food items in general (and in this case, who could blame her?), but it *was* unlike her to be so silent and spacey.

"Tell him, Anna," I demanded, flashing her a

grin that I hoped would snap her out of zipped-lip zone and make her giggle. "Tell Blue that sine and cosine might eventually end up being his best friends!" I added, chuckling as Blue fake punched me across the table.

"Sure, go ahead. I'm done with it anyway," Anna replied, still staring off into nowhere as she gave her plate a gentle shove in my direction.

I exchanged a look with Elizabeth. "Yo, Earth to Anna?" Anna had been acting like the ambassador to Weirdsville all day. And she seemed to be getting worse! Was it something in the food? Not impossible, that's for sure, but I had a feeling there was something else going on with Anna.

I decided to change tack. I mean, I know Anna like the back of my hand, and when something's bugging her, she's hardly an open book. You have to circle around the issue, ask a gazillion questions, try to pick up on when you're getting warmer, and then zero in.

It was time for a little Salvador subtlety.

"How's the play?" I asked casually, giving Elizabeth a knowing nod. Lately Anna's been totally wrapped up in her role as Anita in Sweet Valley Junior High's production of *West Side Story*. So if something was stressing her, chances were it was that. "Are things working out okay?"

I prodded as Anna fiddled with a withered, bruised blob posing as a plum.

"Working out?" She looked puzzled, as if the question was put to her in Mongolian. "Sure, we're just friends."

"Who's just friends?" Elizabeth asked, looking confused. "What are you talking about?"

Suddenly Anna jerked upright in her chair. Her eyes seemed to focus. Apparently she had returned to the land of here and now. "I mean . . . uh . . . Maria and me . . . we're just friends." Okay, she was starting to worry me.

"Who's Maria?" Blue chimed in, scratching at a tuft of bleached hair.

"She's the lead *character* in the play," I explained to Blue, stressing the word *character* as I looked anxiously from Elizabeth to Anna. Anna actually looked kind of miserable, and what she was saying was definitely more than a little on the wacky side. One thing was for sure: She needed something to lighten her up!

"I think being in the play is messing up your brain," I said to Anna, flashing her my goofiest grin. "You should probably let me fill in for you from now on. I think I'd be really good at it." With that, I jumped up, pulled my napkin over my head like a scarf, and started doing the kind of dance I thought they might do in *West Side*

Story. "La la la la la la, America, da da da da da, America." I gave my best rendition of the song I'd heard Anna practice when she was auditioning.

"Shhh!" Elizabeth squealed, standing up and pulling me back to my seat. "We already have one performer at the table. We don't need another one." She grinned at Anna—who didn't even so much as show a hint of a smile. Okay, so maybe my joke was lame, but at least I'd tried! Still, all I got from Anna was one raised eyebrow, and then she folded her arms, looking bored.

"Maybe you've been overrehearsing," Elizabeth said, shooting Anna a sympathetic look.

I nodded, thinking that Elizabeth might be right. After all, Anna had tons of lines and songs and dance steps to learn, and she still had all her schoolwork and work for *Zone*, the online 'zine we'd started a while ago.

"What's this play even about?" Blue asked, yawning and rocking back on his chair. "Is it, like, something watchable, or is it Shakespeare? Because Shakespeare is just not my thing."

"It's the oldest story in the book," Anna murmured in a low voice, looking down at the table. "It's about forbidden love."

"But it does have an upside too," Elizabeth said brightly. "It's also about friendship!"

"Yeah, friendship," Anna said moodily, looking up at me and then at Elizabeth. "And how friendships can be ruined by forbidden love."

"Sounds like an instant downer," Blue said. "Happy ending, I hope?"

"Nope." Anna stared blankly off into space again, and I looked at Elizabeth, who returned my worried glance. Anna wasn't being herself, and there was something she wasn't telling us. Knowing Anna, it would be impossible to squeeze the info out of her, whatever it was.

"Let's change the subject," Elizabeth suggested, trying to get things onto a more cheerful track. Elizabeth and Blue started chatting about *Zone* and workshopping ideas for the next issue. But Anna just shrugged like she didn't care what they talked about. She definitely didn't look much like the usual Anna. The sparkle was gone from her face.

Something *was* upsetting her. I could tell. Her eyes met mine for a second, and she looked away. Whatever it was, she didn't want to talk about it.

And when Anna made up her mind, you could forget about changing it!

Toby's Ten Things I Like about Being an Actor

1. The snack table after Friday rehearsal.
2. The fact that everyone has to sit quietly and listen when I speak.
3. Getting to fight onstage.
4. Getting to pretend I'm Ricky Martin in concert when singing "Tonight."
5. Crying in character is fun. (Not like I'd ever cry out of character or anything.)
6. Getting *two* wardrobe mistresses. (*Two.*)
7. The applause.
8. The applause.
9. Have I mentioned the applause?
10. Anna.

Toby

"Nice work, everyone. Now, let's take it again from the top!" Our choreographer, Ms. Hudson, called out to the dancers after their big tango number.

It was Wednesday afternoon, and I was sitting in the audience seats of the auditorium with Anna and some of the others in the cast, watching the dancers rehearse.

"Aren't they great?" Bianca LaChance commented as the group reassembled and began their dance sequence again.

"Yeah," I replied, smiling at Bianca. Bianca's playing Maria, which basically means she's my leading lady. She's a really cool girl, plus she has the kind of singing voice that makes the hairs on the back of your neck stand up.

Bianca's also extremely pretty, with eyes as big and soft as Natalie Wood's in the movie version of *West Side Story*. She makes my job—falling in love—pretty easy onstage!

But that's just the acting part. As I settled

back into my chair, I glanced next to me at Anna. It would be easier if Anna were playing Maria. Then we'd be spending so much time acting together that maybe I could get her to like me. But she's playing Maria's best friend, so it's not like we get to do any slow-dance numbers together or anything like that!

"Wow," Anna murmured as the dancers kicked into the fast-paced, fancy-footwork section of their number. "Pretty amazing, huh?"

I nodded. The dance numbers were incredible. Ms. Hudson did her best to stay faithful to the original choreography so the production would look as professional as possible. And the dancers were pretty fierce. Mr. Dowd's vision of the play was definitely coming together.

Still, I guess no matter how much I like musicals, my real passion is for straight-up theater. "It's good," I said with a smile, "but it's not *Hamlet*."

Anna looked at me and shook her head, her dimples kicking into gear as she smiled and rolled her eyes. "You and your classics," she teased. "You're a total theater snob!"

"Can I help it if I know quality?" I shot back with a grin. *This is good!* Anna and me—duking it out like old times. We hadn't done this for a while, it seemed, but ever since we met, we've both really liked arguing over theater. Even though it wasn't really arguing. Like, for one thing, I knew for a fact that Anna loved *Hamlet*. We even did a scene from it together once for drama club.

"Oh, come on, Toby!" Anna scoffed. "If you were such a stickler for Shakespeare, you wouldn't be so good at all the singing and dancing. Just admit it—the dramarama stuff's all a big act. You actually love *Cats* and *Phantom of the Opera*!"

I made the international-sign-for-gagging face at her mention of those two cheeseball musicals, but deep down, I was feeling great. *This is more like it!* Things seemed normal again between me and Anna. I wondered if I had even imagined the whole awkward-tension phase.

"So . . . how's everything else going?" I ventured, trying to steer the conversation to other things. I wanted to know as much about Anna as I could. And since we were already talking, I figured now would be a good time to get things onto a more personal note.

Anna looked at me and then quickly turned to watch the dancers. "Larissa is just so awesome," she said, her eyes on the stage. "I could watch her all day long. She's the best dancer of them all, don't you think?"

"Yeah, she's really good," I agreed. And she *was*, definitely. But as I watched Larissa, I couldn't help wondering why Anna had cut me off. Maybe Anna just didn't want to talk about her life or something.

"So are your classes going okay?" I tried again. I wasn't going to give up that easy. If Anna and I were ever going to be close, we had better be able to talk about stuff besides the play.

"Class is fine, I guess," Anna said disinterestedly, still watching the dance number. "And Larissa's doing so much better now that I've been helping her," she said. "I mean, she's so smart, she picks up everything right away. She's not just a talented actress, you know." Anna paused to take in a breath. "Oh . . . and she's also really funny."

What is she? President of Larissa's fan club? "Uh, yeah, of course. Yeah," I muttered, scrutinizing Anna, though I couldn't really see her expression because she had her eyes fixed firmly on Larissa.

This is weird, I thought. Now I was really lost. *First Anna won't talk to me at all, then she's all chatty chatty, and then suddenly she seems to only want to talk about Larissa. Pretty strange too because it's not like I need to be told how great Larissa is. After all, Larissa's my friend!*

What was going on?

Anna

"Dinner in half an hour!" my mom sang up the stairs as I bounded up to my room after rehearsal. "I've made a lentil casserole," she added. "Followed by a strawberry-rhubarb pie. You know, rhubarb's very good for replenishing your energy!"

"Sounds great," I replied, making a face as I scooted around the banister to my room. Rhubarb. It sounded kind of icky, actually, but I didn't want to hurt my mom's feelings. She'd been so depressed about my brother's death for such a long time that seeing her excited about something, even if it was rhubarb, made me really happy. Whenever she snapped out of being sad, she went in the absolute opposite direction. She became full of this crazy energy, and she started cooking all the time. And she became totally obsessed with stuffing me full of weird vegetables and fruits to keep me "at optimal health."

Bed! I thought as I walked into my room and

hurled myself onto my comfy futon. I just felt so wiped out. It wasn't just the rehearsal stuff—which was fun for the most part—but also all that extra Larissa-Toby stuff that added to my exhaustion.

And since Larissa had me on her digging mission with Toby, I felt like I was being stretched on a rack. Torture, medieval style. I mean, I read in history class about the way they used to torture traitors in medieval England, and that's how I was beginning to feel. Especially the traitor part. Because I still felt guilty for having thoughts about Toby even though I was trying really hard to stop thinking about him. Which wasn't easy when it was my job to hang with him and get info for Larissa! What a crazy circle this had turned into. I felt dizzy.

Which made me even happier that I was going to bed for a quick nap before dinner. It was hard to believe that I was this excited to go to sleep.

"Anna!" my mom yelled up in her new-and-improved-mom voice, practically causing me to jump out of my skin. *"Phone!"*

So much for relaxing.

I groaned and dragged my feet back down the stairs to the phone, hoping that whoever it was, I could get rid of them quickly and get back to my cocoon.

"Hey, Anna!" It was Larissa, all breathless and excited. My heart sank. There went my cocooning idea.

"Hi," I said, trying to sound pleasant even though the last thing I felt like was dealing with Larissa right now.

But of course Larissa wasn't about to let me off the hook. She was dying to know what I'd found out about Toby. "I saw you guys talking. Did he say anything?" she blurted out in a rush. "*Dish up,* would you? The suspense is killing me!"

"He thinks you're talented and great," I replied, trying to match her enthusiasm.

"Really?" Larissa practically screamed into my ear. "Are you sure?"

"Things look good," I assured her, hoping against hope that this chat wouldn't last long.

"That's *totally ace,*" Larissa whispered happily. "Because I'm thinking of inviting a bunch of my friends to the park this weekend, and if things look promising with Toby, then I'm going to invite him around as well!"

I couldn't help smiling at Larissa's lingo. She really was one of a kind. And though it was hard, I was glad to know that I was doing everything to protect our friendship. It was definitely worth it.

"Of course you absolutely have to come also!

I need you to carry on with the mission!" Larissa gushed.

I bit my lip. Any other time I would have said yes. But having to endure a day in the park, fishing for answers from Toby, or worse, watching Toby and Larissa flirt, would be too much for me right now. I wasn't ready to watch the flirting, and I was too worn out for the fishing. I needed a weekend away from the whole thing!

"I . . . can't," I answered, rushing to come up with a good excuse. "My mom needs me at home," I mumbled weakly. What a feeble excuse. I knew it wouldn't fly.

"Nonsense," Larissa replied brightly. "It's the weekend. Besides, knowing her, she would want you out in the sun and fresh air!"

"'Optimal health,'" I replied with a sigh and half a smile. Over the past couple of weeks I'd told Larissa all about my mom. I'd have to find a better excuse.

"Um, it's . . . actually the garden," I fumbled, grabbing at straws. "My mom needs my help with her . . . new garden."

Yeah, right! I cringed. That sounded completely weak and stupid, and I knew Larissa wouldn't fall for it either!

"It'll just be for a few hours!" Larissa begged. "Come on, Anna, I really, *really* need you there.

Plus it will be totally fun. We'll probably play either ultimate Frisbee or flag football. Both are good for optimal health!"

I sighed again, giving in. "Uh . . . okay." I didn't want to go, but I knew if I refused to do this for Larissa, she'd be disappointed, and then I'd feel worse for letting her down.

I had no choice. I'd just have to grit my teeth and go.

"Cool!" Larissa chirped happily. "You're the greatest!"

The greatest liar, I thought morosely as I hung up the phone and wandered down the hall. If Larissa only knew how much stuff I was keeping to myself, she'd really hate me. I mean, I'd been trying to put a lid on my feelings for Toby, but I was coming to realize that no matter how hard I tried, I probably couldn't squash them completely.

Like today at rehearsal. Talking to him was just so easy and fun. I had to literally *remind* myself what I was really supposed to talk to him about. Because I was so busy having fun arguing with him, I almost forgot my obligations to Larissa. Some friend I am!

"Ten minutes till dinner," my mom said, looking up at me from the couch as I walked through the TV room.

"Okay," I said, trying to look upbeat and

happy. Actually, what I really wanted to do was sit down on the couch and talk to my mom about everything that was happening. I mean, she's lived a long time—she must have some insight that could be helpful.

I chewed on the inside of my cheek, pausing at the couch, wondering suddenly if maybe I *could* ask my mom's advice.

But who was I kidding? As I watched my mom taking notes from some cooking show, I realized I was in a total dream world if I thought she could be there for me right now.

For starters, she was only just coming out from under a cloud herself. Second, if I told her I was unhappy, she would only worry more. Which would worry me. And third, let's get real: Talking to my mom about Toby would be completely *embarrassing*. Even *picturing* my mom discussing boys is enough to make me double cringe. We just don't have that kind of relationship.

"Everything okay, honey?" Mom asked, looking up from her notes and scrutinizing me from over her reading glasses.

"Everything's fine," I replied, feeling defeated as I left the room.

Yet another person I've lied to, I thought miserably as I walked to the bathroom to wash up for dinner. Of course, everything was *not* fine. The more I tried to force myself not to like Toby, the stronger my crush was growing. But it didn't look like I had much choice. Or maybe I did?

Either way, I was on my own.

A Page from Anna Wang's Poetry Journal, 9:12 p.m., Wednesday

Wasting Away on a Wednesday
What is the matter with me?
Toby is all I can see.
All day I've been moping,
Completely not coping,
And getting no sympathy
A walking misery.

The world is a messy place,
Starvation, disease, the arms race,
But I'm so wrapped up
In my own dumb petty stuff,
~~And it really is a disgrace.~~
Acting like I'm totally spaced.

It's time that I picked up my lip,
Or else ~~I'm gonna~~ those around me might trip!
If I don't clean up my act
And start facing the facts,
~~I will basically end up with zip!~~
My life will be like a sinking ship.

Unless I'm not thinking clearly,
After all, I do like him dearly,
I could ditch Larissa,
Though surely I'd miss'ha
Blah, blah, blech.

Kristin

"Can I have everyone's attention, please?" Ms. McGuire said loudly as the student government assembled for our meeting.

It was normal for everyone to mill around and chat for a few minutes before meetings, but Ms. McGuire's tone completely silenced the room. We all took a seat immediately. I wanted to sit as far away from Ms. McGuire as I could, but I didn't want to look like I was hiding, so I took the seat closest to her. Bethel, who hadn't already had the pleasure of Ms. McGuire's acquaintance, sat right next to me.

"My name is Ms. McGuire," our new adviser said energetically, adjusting her glasses and unsnapping a smart black briefcase onto the table in front of her. "As most of you already know, I'll be taking over from Ms. Kern as adviser to the student government." *Yes, we already know*. I couldn't believe this was actually happening. "I'm hoping that you're all as excited about this as I am." *Right.*

Ms. McGuire stopped for a moment and gave the room a brief catch-it-if-you-can smile. I couldn't speak for anyone else, but I wouldn't have exactly called it a friendly smile. More like an obligation. Like we were at a business meeting and she was an important client instead of an adviser meant to be helping us.

"We'll probably be taking the next few weeks to get to know each other a bit better, but in the meantime let's get right down to work." She started smoothing the wrinkles out of her skirt. Not that there were any wrinkles to be smoothed.

"Kristin? Why don't you lead by giving us a breakdown of what you see as the student government's top-five upcoming priorities?"

Ms. McGuire regarded me intently. The room was unusually silent and focused, and I swallowed hard, wishing that by some miracle Ms. Kern would walk through the door and announce that it had all been a mistake, that things with her family were fine and everything could go back to normal.

But *that* wasn't going to happen! Right now Ms. Kern was probably clearing out the last bookshelf in her office or going through last-minute administrative affairs with the principal.

Top-five priorities! I scrambled through my various agenda books and lists, my hands shaking. I could feel everyone's eyes on me. As president, it was up to me to lead the way. But I was a nervous wreck! It felt like the room was full of sparks, like the air before a thunderstorm.

Top-five priorities! Right now my number one would be hotfooting it out of this room!

"Well," I began, clearing my throat and then trailing off into nowhere. I knew what our priorities were, but I felt so caught off guard that my brain started spinning and short-circuiting. "There's, um, well, the, uh, book fair," I struggled, trying to keep my voice strong and steady.

"But isn't that in May?" Ms. McGuire replied, glancing down at her notebook. "What about the upcoming spring dance? And fund-raising for the next semester? Have you brainstormed any ideas for those things yet?"

"Uh . . . no. Not fully, I mean," I answered, trying somehow to still sound capable instead of like the scatterbrain that she probably thought I was. "We have ideas in the works, but nothing's been finalized either for the dance or the budget fund-raisers," I added.

"Hmmm." Ms. McGuire looked miffed and

fiddled with her fancy Mont Blanc pen, clicking it over and over, a sound that was doing nothing for the state of my nerves. "Don't you think we'd better step up the pace, then?" she challenged. "Time is of the essence, students! Responsibility is key!"

As the others all nodded and started scribbling things down—probably just trying to look busy—I felt my face begin to burn again. It's horrible being so fair skinned because I blush so easily.

Ms. McGuire was making me feel awful. *Ms. Kern* always made feel like I was on top of things. She would have had no problem with the fact that all the details of our goals weren't entirely smoothed out yet. She understood how hard it was to be 100 percent on target with everything at this stage of the game.

"We do have some solid ideas for raising funds, and we do have our dance themes narrowed down." Bethel spoke up suddenly. Was it my imagination, or was she sitting up straighter than normal?

"We have three top themes for the dance," Bethel continued, tucking a stray braid behind her ear in one efficient move. "Roman Feast, 1920s Flapper Fest, and Fantasy Island."

I could have told her that! I thought, annoyed

that Bethel had suddenly taken the reins. I mean, if Ms. McGuire had asked what our ideas for the dance were, I could have told her off the top of my head! But she'd wanted final decisions, not a list of possibilities.

Still, it seemed she was happy with what Bethel was giving her. And suddenly it seemed like the whole group was becoming more focused. People started offering their input on the dance ideas. This was usually something I had to *force* them to do, but now it seemed like I was the only one with nothing to offer!

"Lots of good ideas, lots to think about," Ms. McGuire said matter-of-factly after some more brainstorming. "Now, what about the fund-raisers and facts and figures? Kristin. Give me a stat report. How much have we raised for the dance so far, and how much more do we need?"

What we have *is a problem!* my reflex inner voice shouted up at me. *What we* need *is Ms. Kern!* But that kind of thinking wasn't going to get me very far.

"We, uh, have a, uh, projected—I mean, targeted—um, amount of . . . money." I blathered like a senseless idiot as Ms. McGuire fixed me with her piercing, cool-eyed stare and drummed her perfectly manicured fingernails on the table.

"We've got an account balance of a hundred dollars," Bethel interjected, looking over my shoulder at the budget figures in my notebook. "But we still need another hundred and fifty to meet our total estimated costs for the dance budget."

"Any ideas as to how to get that taken care of?" Ms. McGuire inquired as I sat dumbfounded and annoyed at Bethel and myself and Ms. McGuire all in one hot, panicky, face-burning second. I knew the figures, and I should have been the one telling Ms. McGuire. I guess I just hadn't really known that *that* was what she was asking me for. *Stat report, facts and figures.* The woman spoke in tongues!

Either that or I was too upset and too dense to understand even simple things. And whichever one of those two options was correct, it didn't exactly make me feel good.

While Bethel and the others all pitched in ideas and the room buzzed with a drone of energetic voices, I felt myself close up inside. I started fantasizing about the earth opening up and swallowing me right then and there.

Will this ever end? I hadn't started out the meeting feeling incompetent, but I certainly did now. Because clearly I was no good to anyone in this room.

As I sat there, feeling about as valuable and appreciated as an extra on a movie set, there was only one thing that I felt clear on: I was blowing it. In a major way. In front of everyone.

Salvador

"So did Big Noise make a big noise today, or are you guys actually getting close to making some music?" Anna asked from the kitchen counter, where she was halfheartedly nibbling on one of my grandmother's legendary, ultimate-best-in-the-world, fresh-from-the-oven oatmeal cookies.

I swung onto a stool next to Anna and made a face at her. "For your information, the band is really hot right now," I said, grabbing a fistful of cookies from the baking tray on the kitchen counter.

That was no lie either. We'd had some hiccups to start with, but the band I was in with Blue, Brian, and Damon had really started to pick up lately. We finally had some good songs, and more important, we were actually having fun!

"Hmmph," Anna said, looking less than impressed as I sang a lyric from our newest song, "Catch Her If You Can." "Maybe I need to hear the whole thing to fully appreciate it," she finished, taking a swig from her glass of milk.

Salvador

"Well, I like it," the Doña said, removing another tray of cookies from the oven and beaming. "I think it really rocks out!"

"Right on, Doña!" I laughed, and even moody Anna cracked a tiny smile. "At least *someone* here believes in me," I said, shooting Anna a meaningful glance as my grandma went back into the sitting room to her knitting.

"Well, maybe the Doña's hearing isn't quite as good as mine," Anna replied, brushing crumbs from the countertop.

Of course I knew Anna was just kidding, but there was something in her tone that bothered me. I don't know how to describe it—coldness, maybe? Whatever it was, it wasn't typical of the Anna I know.

But it was typical of the Anna I'd been dealing with over the past few days. *It's time to get to the bottom of this,* I decided as Anna made lazy shapes in the remaining cookie crumbs with her fingernails. Whatever was eating her, I was going to get it out of her the old-fashioned way.

Like, the blunt and obvious way.

"What's up, Anna? You've been acting weird all week. Talk to me."

"What do you mean, weird?" Anna replied dismissively.

"I mean *weird* weird. *Distracted* weird. Sulky, pouty, *quiet* weird—"

Anna fidgeted in her chair and stared down at the cookie crumbs, biting her lip. Finally, after a long silence, she looked up at me. "Okay." She held up her hands in defeat just as I was opening my mouth to try again.

I stopped, surprised that she'd given in so easily. Usually it took a lot more than that to get Anna Wang to give in.

"Okay, you're right," Anna admitted in a small voice. "Something *is* bugging me. But I can't really talk about it."

I settled back into my seat, disappointed. I could tell by the look in Anna's eyes that she really *did* want to talk about it. I paused midway between cookie bites, plotting my next move. "Well, if you don't want to talk about it, I certainly wouldn't want to drag it out of you."

We sat in silence for a while. Well, except for the munching noises coming from my mouth. Anna continued to plug away at her cookie-crumb concoction.

"More milk?" I asked.

"All right, I'll tell you, but then you have to stop bugging me," she blurted out.

"Well, you don't have to tell me if you don't want to, Anna." *Tell me already.*

"Sal," she said, in a tone that meant I wasn't fooling her with my childish mind games. "Toby is really bugging me, and I don't know what to do."

Toby? As in Mr. Wonderful Toby? *That* surprised me, I have to say. I mean, ever since she'd met him, Anna had given me nothing but glowing reports about the gifted, talented, hilarious Toby. It was even slightly sickening how much she liked the guy.

"I guess the problem is that I like him. I mean, as more than a friend." She raised her eyebrows at me, then continued. "But Larissa also likes him, so we have a . . . situation." Anna sighed and bit her thumbnail while my brain spun with the news.

So *that's* what this was about! It took a moment for me to digest Anna's story, but as she filled me in, I slowly got the picture. She was in a classic love triangle. I knew from my own experience that there was nothing like the old love triangle to get in the way of a good time.

"I feel totally trapped," Anna admitted glumly, pushing a strand of black hair from her cheek. "I guess that's how you and Liz felt when . . . when all that stuff happened," Anna murmured, looking up at me warily. "Now I understand how hard that must have been for you two."

So *that's* what was going on at lunch yesterday!

"It's okay," Anna assured me as I looked at the floor, feeling bad about the whole Elizabeth thing all over again. And as Anna explained to me that she really wasn't still hurt and upset about what had happened with me and Elizabeth, I couldn't help feeling a flash of guilt zigzagging through my guts.

"I'm sorry—I didn't bring it up to make you feel bad. I was just trying to tell you that now I understand what it must have been like for you."

I got up to get more milk from the fridge, my thoughts ticking away on the recent developments. A bunch of unwanted memories popped up all over the place. Me kissing Elizabeth. Me all confused and then kissing Anna and *then* going out with her, even though I really liked Elizabeth. Anna crying and Elizabeth acting like she hated me. It was a miracle any of us had managed to stay friends.

"And that's why I'm trying to be extra careful that I don't ever do that to someone else," Anna continued.

"Like Larissa, you mean." I flipped the lid of the milk carton and refilled my glass. Awkward conversations make me thirsty, and I drained my glass in one swallow and refilled again.

"I guess I feel pretty stumped, though," Anna confessed gloomily. "I just don't know *how* to be a good friend to Larissa without hurting myself in the process. Maybe I should tell her how I feel."

"Huh?" Call me slow, but all this stuff about friends liking friends was kind of playing with my head.

"Sal? Are you still with me?" Anna waved from across the kitchen. Guess I'd been pulling the old glassy-eyed stare. Not unlike Anna at lunch yesterday, come to think of it.

"I don't want to hurt Larissa. And I've tried to make myself stop liking Toby. But I haven't been successful at it yet. So maybe I should just tell her what's been going on."

Anna looked pleadingly at me. I could see her dilemma, sure, and I knew she wanted advice, but there was this other, kind of strange feeling all mixed up in the sympathy I had for Anna's situation. This funny, kind of pinching, hot feeling. Kind of a jealous-type feeling.

"So which is it? Help Larissa get Toby, or tell her the truth about my feelings for him?" Anna demanded as I shifted uncomfortably on my stool, wondering if my jealousy would show up as a greenish tint on my skin.

Trust me, I don't *like* Anna as a girlfriend or anything. We've been through that whole saga, and it didn't pan out. So we're best friends, nothing more. But I guess a part of me also didn't want her liking anyone else.

Wow! I guess this was *exactly* what Anna

must have felt like when Elizabeth and I were together.

I shifted again, weirded out by the fact that I could feel a little bit of what it must have been like to be in Anna's shoes. *Ouch.*

"Sal! Help me," Anna practically shouted. "What should I do?"

I swallowed, wondering what I should tell her. I was Anna's best friend, and she'd probably take my advice to heart—so I wanted to give her the *right* advice. The thing was, I wasn't sure I could keep my jealousy from getting in the way.

I gave Anna a sympathetic smile, trying to look as helpful and caring and unbiased as possible. "I think you should leave Toby alone," I offered. "For Larissa's sake."

Anna

"Who are you leaving alone?" the Doña queried breezily as she marched into the kitchen to refill her teacup. "And who is this Clarissa?"

Great! I clenched my jaw and squeezed my hands together as the Doña bustled past me to the teakettle on the stove. My ears burned as if someone had put *them* on the hot plate! I mean, it was bad enough having to have this awkward talk with Salvador, but now it seemed the Doña had picked up on the conversation, and I was totally embarrassed.

I chided myself, regretting the fact that I'd ever opened my big mouth instead of just shutting up about Toby. But it was too late for regrets. The Doña was scrutinizing me with her piercing black eyes, tapping her fingers while the kettle boiled, and smiling her kindly—but oh-so-curious—smile.

"It's Larissa," I corrected her, and cleared my throat. "She's, uh, a friend of a friend." My ears were still flaming as I struggled and failed to think up a cover for my story. *Punishment,* I told myself. *I guess this is what I get for making jokes about the Doña's hearing!*

"Friend of a friend," the Doña repeated, nodding thoughtfully. "I'm sorry to eavesdrop, but it did sound very interesting. Something about lying and telling the truth."

"Yes," I answered hastily, trying to look confident. "It's my friend . . . *Hannah* . . . ," I blathered, looking at Salvador and wondering how much of our conversation the Doña had heard. I cursed myself for coming up with such a weak name. I guess I just had to hope the Doña would buy it.

For his part, Salvador didn't look too concerned. In fact, he looked kind of distracted, like he was trying to work out an algebra problem in his head.

"This . . . Hannah . . . she's having a problem with Larissa?" the Doña pressed as she opened a tin of jasmine tea and carefully measured leaves into a tiny silver spoon.

"Yeah, it's kind of a . . . boy problem." I tried to look away from the Doña's eyes. She had this kind of intelligent been-there, done-that look about her, and I felt bad making up stories about "Hannah." I was turning into a regular liar these days.

"Ah, yes." The Doña gave a sharp, severe nod as she sealed the tea tin. "Boys are a terrible problem. Always have been, always will be."

I giggled, even though my ears were still doing a flame number on my head. At least I could still laugh at the situation—especially the way the Doña had put it. She'd totally hit the nail on the head.

And laughing did make me feel a bit better. A little more loosened up or something. So before long I was spilling "Hannah's" story to the Doña. Carefully, of course. I mean, I love the Doña. Even though she can be a bit . . . how can I put this delicately . . . nosy sometimes, I know she means well. But that didn't mean I wanted her to know that these were *my* dark secrets.

Luckily she seemed to have bought the Hannah angle. Now maybe I could get her take on things without giving myself away.

"So your friend has found herself between a rock and a wall," the Doña mused, narrowing her eyes in concentration.

"Exactly." I smiled, and Salvador, apparently paying attention now, grinned and rolled his eyes at me. The Doña spoke English perfectly, but she sometimes mixed her metaphors together, and it was pretty funny.

Anyway, she was right! Rock, wall, hard place, whatever, I was definitely *stuck.*

"When you're stuck in between two alternatives and neither is quite right, it can seem impossible to make a move." The Doña jabbed her finger in the air and then fell silent. "It can be tough," she continued seriously. "Especially without all the facts of the matter."

"What facts?" Salvador asked. He'd broken out of his trance now and was rummaging through the fridge.

"Well, this Hannah doesn't know what Toby feels about *her!* A very important piece of information," she continued. "Without which our friend Hannah *cannot* move forward!"

I sat up straighter on my stool. The Doña was right. Of course. I'd been so caught up in the problem that I'd missed a big part of it. I *didn't* really know what Toby thought of me. Although I could pretty much guess the answer. I'd seen him with Larissa, and they definitely got along really well together. . . .

"If *I* were Hannah, I would find that out first. And if Hannah finds out that Toby likes her too, then she should be honest with her friend Larissa."

"Really?" I blurted out loudly, a little too enthusiastically for someone who was meant to just be a *friend* of "Hannah's."

"Of course," she replied as the kettle began to whistle. "Honesty, my dear, is *always* the best policy."

"Not always," Salvador argued as he emerged from the fridge with a wedge of cheddar cheese and an avocado. "Like if someone is dying of cancer and they only have three weeks to live. Should the doctor tell them they only have three weeks? No!" he concluded triumphantly, setting the cheese down on the counter and grabbing a big knife. "Because the truth would *hurt*."

Okay, so maybe no one was dying here, but Salvador did have a point. And though my ears had stopped burning, my head was starting to pound with the combination of the now screeching kettle and all the confusion inside me. Lies. Truth. As far as I was concerned, they *both* hurt.

"No, Salvador," the Doña responded vehemently. "Better to have the truth hurt than to have a lie any day of the week. This Hannah, she has a right to know Toby's feelings. Toby has a right to know hers. And Larissa has a right to know what's going on too!"

Except that she'll hate me no matter what! I thought miserably as the Doña turned off the hot plate and poured steaming water into her china teacup.

"Well, I think a good friend is one who *protects* her friend from the truth," Salvador retorted, cutting a hunk of cheese.

"The truth shall set you free," the Doña shot back, following up with a shrewd grin.

"Ignorance is bliss." Salvador smiled gleefully as he carved up the avocado.

Help! I thought weakly as I watched the Doña and Salvador slam it out. It was like being at Wimbledon or something. Two pros on opposite sides of the net.

Who was I supposed to believe? The Doña's advice sounded really good . . . until Salvador put in his two cents!

And if lies saved the day and truth set you free, then why did I feel so trapped? I sighed as the pros continued to ace each other, shot for shot. It was one for one between the Doña and Salvador, but where did that leave me?

Now, that's a riddle I *could* solve—*nowhere!*

Anna's Ten Reasons *Not* to Like Toby

1. Birthmark (or mole??) above left ear.
2. Attention hogger.
3. Dental problems.
4. Tries to get away with Larissa-isms like "blooming" and "brilliant."
5. Does not like *Cats.*
6. Does not like cats (therefore would not pet Whiskers if at my house).
7. We have too much in common: drama, like same food, laugh at same things. (Opposites attract. Similar is boring.)
8. Distracts me in rehearsal by making goofy faces during serious scenes; i.e., bad influence . . .
9. Allergic to peanuts (means no sharing Fluffernutters, a necessary act of bonding for *any* relationship).
10. Not liking him will save my friendship with Larissa.

Anna

"Bye, I'll call when we're done!" I slammed the car door and waved good-bye to my mom at the entrance to Sweet Valley's biggest park, Rolling Meadows Green. It was a beautiful Saturday morning, and any other time I would have totally been up for some fun in the park, but as I walked through the gates, my heart sank more and more with each step.

Here goes . . . I took a deep breath as I spotted the group hanging on the lawn. Could I handle this? I was still so mixed up over Larissa and Toby, and days of thinking had gotten me nowhere. I didn't have a clue what to do. *Except pretend to be happy,* I told myself, pasting a grin on my face as I neared Larissa, Toby, and a bunch of Larissa's friends, sitting near a giant oak tree.

"Great shorts, Anna," Bianca complimented me as I walked up to join the group. "Are they new?"

"Not really," I replied brightly. The truth was,

they were brand-spanking-new red board shorts that I had groveled and begged and pleaded with my mom for.

I'd never worn them before. But I didn't want to look like I was getting all dressed up for a morning in the park. Not with Larissa in cutoffs and all the others in old khakis. I mean, it could make me look a bit suspicious. Not that I *had* picked the pants out to impress Toby or anyone else. I just wanted to look . . . nice, I guess.

"Yeah, those are brilliant," Toby chirped, appearing from out of nowhere, and I felt my face flame up bloodred to match the pants as he looked me up and down. Besides the fact that he was trying too hard to sound British, he was as adorable as ever.

Stop being an idiot! I ordered myself, bugged that Toby's compliment meant something to me and doubly bugged that I was beginning to feel all flushed and sweaty palmed. How would I get through the morning if I didn't chill out? By moving away from Toby, that's how.

I headed toward the group of girls seated by Larissa. "I'm so completely psyched that you came!" Larissa exclaimed, reaching up to squeeze my hand.

Larissa did look psyched—but I doubted it was simply my appearance at the scene that was giving her that glow. I think it had a bit more to do with Toby being there than anything else.

"Make sure you talk to him," she hissed in my ear, nudging me and jerking her head in Toby's direction. "Okay?"

I nodded, looking anywhere *but* at Toby. I would do what Larissa wanted. Eventually. But right now I was just trying to assimilate and get my bearings. After all, it could be a *very* long day. . . .

"Hey, gang, what's cooking?" It was Pete Kelly, who'd sauntered up to join us. Pete was one of the best dancers in *West Side Story,* and he was with three others from the cast—Bianca, Sara Carnes, and Miguel Santos. "Brought the football like you asked." Pete grinned and held a football up above his head.

"I brought snacks," someone else interjected.

Before long we were all sitting on the grass, drinking soda and eating Doritos, while Larissa and Bianca ran around the grass, planting twigs for flag football.

"She's like the Energizer Bunny," Toby commented, settling next to me on the grass and pointing in Larissa's direction. "Never runs out of energy."

"I hope I can keep up," I replied, only half kidding. I mean, I like sports. I'm not completely uncoordinated, and running around on a nice day was hardly going to kill me. But football—flag or no flag—well, let's just say I wouldn't know what to do with a football if my life depended on it.

"Okay, two teams, everyone!" Larissa yelled, and marshaled everyone into lines.

Within a few moments we had our team. Me, Larissa, Pete, Sara, and Miguel were on the same team. We all joined together in a huddle.

"We take no prisoners," Larissa yelled in a mock-coach voice after going over the rules. "Victory is our quest, and we shall prevail!"

"You said it, sister!" Pete responded emphatically, and we all cheered and whooped.

And right then I guess I just started getting caught up in all the silliness. Somehow from the moment I heard everyone cheering it was as if all my troubles got lifted into the air right along with the sounds of our voices. Suddenly it was just me and a bunch of my friends kidding around and acting like a pile of idiots.

"We rule!" Larissa screeched as Sara scored a touchdown.

"Not for long!" Toby yelled back. He grinned at Larissa and made a face at me, and I laughed. Toby was drenched with sweat, and his mop of brown curls was standing up on end like Albert Einstein's. It was definitely a sight to make you laugh, even if you were so winded, you couldn't breathe.

"You better watch out," I teased Toby as we got ready to play. "We might end up ruffling your fancy do!"

The more I laughed, the easier the game got. I'd arrived at the park all nervous and dreading having to deal with Toby and Larissa, but out there on the grass all I could think of was the game and making my teammates happy.

Which was probably why I got so excited when I actually *caught* the ball after a good half hour of being easily the weakest, most out-of-it player on the team. But suddenly everyone was cheering and I was making a real run for it. Except that I couldn't figure out which way I was meant to be running. *So just run!* I thought wildly, sputtering into giggles as I struggled for breath. The whole game was so totally unfocused and silly, but it was a total blast!

From my left side I heard a sudden burst of sound. "Whoa!" Then before I could identify who it was making the sound or what was happening, my answer came in the form of a major thwack to my side.

The next moment I was lying on the grass with a mouthful of leaves and a big weight on top of me as heavy as an anchor. I looked up, brushing mown grass from my face to find myself looking straight into *Toby's* eyes!

"I'm really sorry, Anna," Toby apologized, staring down at me and rubbing his cheek gingerly before rolling onto his side. "Guess I didn't see you coming."

"It's, um, it's . . . ," I muttered, flustered as I tried to untangle my limbs and straighten my clothes. "It's okay," I finished as Toby's face swam into close-up focus again.

He peered at me, concerned. "Are you sure I didn't hurt you? I must weigh twice as much as you!"

"No, really." I looked away and brushed off my T-shirt. My throat felt suddenly dry, and my heart was pounding so loudly, I was afraid Toby might hear it. I guess it was a combination of the fall and Toby's deep brown eyes peering into my face.

It was all a bit overwhelming, and I felt kind of woozy.

"Let me help you up," Toby offered, holding out his hand as he stood up.

But I sprang to my feet on my own, eager to get back to the others so that he wouldn't see how discombobulated I was. It was embarrassing, and I just wanted to get away from him before I weirded him out.

"I'm fine," I insisted. "I don't break *that* easily!"

Toby gave me a really sweet smile then. He has this kind of lopsided smile and really big white teeth, and his smiles always stretch all the way up to include his eyes. I like that. Plus he looked really caring and kept apologizing even though it was totally not necessary.

"Let's move it," I shouted to the team, giving them a thumbs-up as they gathered around me.

The fall had been a little setback. I had been doing a fairly decent job of pushing away my feelings for Toby. But seeing him up close with that concerned, kind look in his eyes . . . I admit, it had made me feel pretty wobbly. Even more wobbly than when he'd actually literally knocked me off my feet.

But it was just a *little* setback, and I had no intention of letting it sidetrack me from my goals: to have fun with Larissa and everyone else—and to *not* think about Toby.

"You ready?" Larissa yelled.

"Ready!" we all screamed back as Bianca kicked the ball.

And I was. Ready to let the day roll along. No more wobbly moments—we had a game to win!

Toby

"Beverage, immediately!" I gasped as I fell onto the grass next to the cooler, panting. Flag football was quite a workout, even after all the singing and dancing I'd been doing for the play.

"Thanks, Maria," I said gratefully as my *West Side Story* costar, Bianca, tossed me the Mountain Dew that I was too exhausted to reach for. "No wonder I love you so much," I kidded. Bianca decked me playfully on the side of my head and scooted off to hang with the other girls.

Now, this is the life, I thought happily after draining the ice-cold soda and settling back onto the grass. It *was* the perfect day. I'd played out my guts in the game, which was a great stress outlet. I'd had a really great time goofing around with Larissa and all of her friends. And even better, I'd gotten to hang with Anna—outside of school, outside of the play. Which was pretty cool.

Especially the part when I fell on her. Not that I meant to knock her over or anything. *That* part wasn't cool, obviously. But she wasn't hurt, and I'd never really been up close and personal with Anna. Close enough to pick up that her hair smelled like lemon shampoo. Close enough to see that she has these really neat flecks of orange in her eyes. And really cute, tiny ears, like perfect seashells . . .

Ugh! I really am turning into a sappy romantic! I thought. But I couldn't help it. Maybe it was all the musical theater. Maybe singing all those mushy love songs as Tony had turned me into a softie. . . . But if it led to falling on girls whose hair smelled *that* good, then maybe the mushy stuff wasn't that bad after all.

"Can you open this, Toby?" Larissa broke into my thoughts. I sat up on my elbows as she crouched next to me and held out a big bottle of Coke. "Untwistable," she said as I took the bottle. "And it's an emergency. I'm parched."

"I read you," I replied with a smile as I twisted the lid hard. "Watch it!" I added, holding the bottle away from us as the soda suddenly fizzed up and spilled down my hand.

"Thanks!" Larissa flashed me a grateful grin and grabbed the bottle, then darted off to grab cups.

I wiped my soda-sticky hands on my T-shirt and did a mental rewind, back to the moment when Anna and I were lying on the grass. Did I imagine it, or was there something going on with her too? Something more than just friendly vibes?

You won't know until you ask her! something inside me suddenly piped up. And that's when I realized what I had to do—take action. Not telling Anna what I felt about her wasn't working. Maybe the reason that she and I seemed to be having all these weird, uncomfortable moments was that I wasn't telling her how I felt.

As someone somewhere (King Lear? Hamlet? Elvis Presley?) once said, "Nothing ventured, nothing gained!"

Anna

"I'll call you later," Larissa said meaningfully, her eyes glinting as Sara's mom revved the engine of her car. "Don't forget to do your *homework!*" she added with a wink as Toby came up beside me.

"Okay," I murmured as Larissa grabbed me and gave me a quick, forceful hug before scooting into the car.

"Byeee!" Larissa waved, and the car sped off, leaving me alone with Toby. The last place I wanted to be!

"You really don't need to wait," I said to Toby, gesturing in the direction of his bike, chain locked to a pole next to the park gates. "Go," I urged him. "Really, it's okay. My mom's never late."

"Nope." Toby grinned and shifted to sit on the park wall. "I wasn't brought up that way," he added, running a hand through his curls. "Chivalry isn't dead, you know!"

I wish it were! I found myself thinking as I

blinked at Toby and made an effort to look pleased, shrugging to cover up the panic I felt growing inside me.

I knew exactly what Larissa meant by "homework." Why else would she have been so eager to hightail it out of the park with the others if she hadn't wanted me to be alone with Toby? Alone so I could ask him *the* question. Alone so that I could find out whether he really liked her or not.

I groaned inwardly and climbed up onto the wall next to Toby. Larissa, Toby, Sara, and I had been the last to leave the park. And it had been really fun, lying on the grass and shooting the breeze, just the four of us. I'd even felt comfortable around Toby and kind of relaxed, like my old self. Until Larissa started shooting me meaningful glances and asking Sara if she could get a ride home with Sara's mom.

I knew what that meant. And I also knew that Toby would be a real gentleman and wait for me to go home before jumping on his bicycle and heading off. That's the kind of guy he is.

Unfortunately, at this particular moment, Toby's niceness was just making things more difficult for me because there was no way out of the situation. This was *the* moment, the perfect opportunity for me to act like Larissa's true friend and do what she needed me to do.

If I could do it.

"Did you have fun today?" Toby asked me as I jiggled my dangling feet against the park wall.

"Yeah, I really did," I replied, twirling my silver pinkie ring around and around my finger. I *had* had a good time. Despite everything, the day had turned out to be way better than I thought it could have.

"Do you think those grass stains will come out?" Toby asked, sounding apologetic as he pointed at a green skid mark on the pocket of my new red board shorts.

"I don't care—it was worth it. . . ." *Oops!* I bit my lip, cursing myself for being so stupid. I guess I was so fixated on the close-up image I had of Toby's eyes (with eyelashes long enough to run a marathon on) that I'd just spoken automatically, as if he wasn't there to hear me! "I mean . . . the game was worth a few stains," I bumbled, trying to cover up.

I'd been doing a lot of that lately. Covering up. And it was getting to be a real strain on me. At that moment I'd have given anything to just say what was on my mind. But I couldn't.

So do the next best thing, I ordered myself. *Say what's on* Larissa's *mind. Ask the question! Prove that you're a friend!*

Anna

My head felt like it was about to split with the force of all the commands I was giving myself. Part of me was screaming at myself to do what Larissa wanted. And another part of me just wanted to get up and run. Then there was the part of me that wanted to ask Toby how he felt about me. But I could never do that.

I took a deep breath. It was now or never.

"Do you like Larissa?" I asked Toby, looking him full in the face. No more beating around the bush. I had to be straight up.

"Of course I do," Toby replied instantly, and my heart sank like a stone. I couldn't help it. I wanted to be happy for her. But I was only human. "Larissa's great," Toby continued, running a hand through his hair.

Larissa's great? I wasn't exactly sure what he meant by that. It certainly didn't sound like a declaration of undying love. On the other hand, maybe I just wasn't getting his meaning because I didn't want to.

"I mean, do you *like* her, like her," I rephrased the question.

"You mean *like* her?" His voice crackled. *Why does he have to be so cute?* I wondered. *Even when he's breaking my heart.*

"Yes. I mean *like* her, like her," I clarified impatiently. *Can we get this over with already so I can just go home and lock myself in the bathroom for a year or two?* I held my breath as I waited for his response. I wanted to look at the ground while he answered me, but I knew that would give me away, so I kept staring directly at him.

"No, uh . . ." Toby fumbled. "I mean, I do like her, but not in *that* way." Now *he* was looking down.

I was kind of shocked. That wasn't the answer I was expecting! I had been so positive that he liked her, I hadn't considered any other possibility. Relief washed over me, but I also felt so bad for Larissa that I almost wished Toby had answered the question differently.

"I, um, I like someone else, though," Toby said nervously, still ducking his head and looking kind of shy and awkward.

I wondered who the "someone else" could be. There was always Bianca. *Of course!* Why hadn't I thought of that before? They were playing a couple in the play, and everyone knows that actors blur the lines between the stage and real life. It's only natural. . . .

"I like you, Anna."

He'd said it so quietly, I thought I'd imagined it. But then I looked up at Toby, and I could tell from his eyes that he'd just told me the one thing I wanted to hear most in the world.

And in a way, also the *last* thing I wanted to hear!

I sat there staring numbly at him while he peeled the label off his soda bottle. What could I say to him?

My mind went blank. Toby continued on his peeling mission—I could tell he was trying to get the label all off in one piece. I wanted to tell him to wait until the bottle dried to make it easier, but I didn't want to seem like I was ignoring his comment.

This was getting ridiculous. I had to respond, but I didn't know what to say. I certainly couldn't tell him the truth—that I liked him too—because that would make me a hypocrite after all the anger I'd felt toward Elizabeth and Salvador about them liking each other behind my back. I couldn't do to Larissa exactly what I'd sworn I would never even do to my worst enemy.

But then again, pretending I didn't like Toby wasn't an option either. That would be almost worse. I was tired of lying.

"So, um, what do you think?" Toby mumbled nervously as I sat there, gaping at him. I was still in total shock—Toby liked *me*. Sure, I'd hoped that he liked me, I'd even thought I'd noticed some signs that he did, but now that he had actually admitted his feelings, I couldn't really believe it!

Think . . . think! I implored myself as Toby dug away at that label. I had to say *some*thing. After all, it had obviously taken courage for him to admit this to me. And he deserved some sort of answer—anything was better than silence. *Help!*

Just then, by some miracle, help arrived: in the form of a red Mazda and a mom—my mom—driving it.

Thank goodness! I jumped off the wall and grabbed my backpack from the grass, wondering when I'd ever—in the history of my entire life—been this excited to get picked up by my mom.

"Sorry," I murmured to Toby, barely looking him in the eye as my mom slowed in front of us. "Gotta go."

But as I opened the car door, slid onto the cool leather seat, and felt the first flood of relief hit me, I also felt an overwhelming wave of regret. And while I watched Toby's figure growing smaller as the car picked up speed, I wondered whether my escape route would just bring me more trouble in the end.

Either way, I knew that whatever happened next, my friendships with Toby and Larissa were about to change.

E-mail Forward from Elizabeth to Anna—9:00 p.m., Sunday

Anna: check this out. Jess fwded it to me, and I'm fwding it to you. I hate chain letters, but I couldn't resist this one! Put your name on bottom of the list and pass on!—Liz

Fwd: The Chain of Friendship

Take a moment to stop and think about your friends. Friends are the most valuable thing in the world. Love comes and goes, luck comes and goes, money comes and goes, beauty and success—these things too will fade with time and circumstance. But your friend is there forever. Treasure your friend and never forget that a true friend is hard to find. Don't take your friendship for granted!

If you've received this e-mail, it's because someone thinks of you as a good and loyal friend.

Now, take a moment and think of another special friend whom you really trust and appreciate. With this e-mail make a solemn vow to *always* be there for that friend. Then add your name and forward this to your treasured friend. . . . And when you, the recipient of this e-mail, get this, look down the list and see the chain of friendship! Don't break the chain! And remember, someone thinks you're a gem of a friend!

Kristin

"I think she's a witch," I told my best friend, Lacey Frells, emphatically as we walked toward room 103 for algebra, which is the first class we have on Mondays.

By "she" I was of course referring to Ms. McGuire. All weekend I'd been going over and over the student-government meeting in my head, looking for ways to see things differently. But the more I looked back on that hideous meeting, the more I was convinced that Ms. McGuire was *not* a very nice person.

And it felt good to tell Lacey that. I'd known Lacey since the second grade, and if anyone would understand, it would be her. She knew me almost as well as I knew myself!

"Wow," Lacey remarked, turning to give me the famous Lacey look—a quick but expert once-over, where she basically looks you up and down (keeping her tiny, freckled, ski-jump nose in the air) and assesses you in a millisecond. "You're really not in a good mood these days, are you?"

"What does *that* have to do with anything?" I snapped as we rounded the corner and made for Mr. Wilfred's classroom. I was annoyed. Where was the sympathy, support, and understanding Lacey should be giving me as my oldest friend under the sun? I've been there for her whenever she's needed me, but now she was just treating me as if I'd woken up on the wrong side of the bed!

In other words, Lacey was acting like my problem with Ms. McGuire wasn't real—or wasn't a very big deal.

But when I spotted Bethel headed toward me, I suddenly saw a way to prove that the problem *wasn't* just in my mind.

Bethel had been very vocal during last week's meeting, and it had definitely annoyed me when she kept speaking up, giving Ms. McGuire my answers for me. But after reflecting on that for a while, I realized that Bethel must have been as nervous and shaken by Ms. McGuire's sharpness as I was. And while some people (like me) clam up when they're on edge, others (like Bethel) babble.

"Hey, Bethel," I greeted her as she came toward us. "Some meeting last week, huh?" I added neutrally. I mean, I didn't want to just come out and ask her if she agreed that Ms. McGuire was a witch. Because if she didn't agree, then I'd look bad. But I did want to feel her out and see what she really thought.

And maybe now, away from Ms. McGuire's eagle eye, I'd get Bethel's honest opinion.

"Yeah, what do *you* think of the famous Ms. McGuire?" Lacey piped in. I immediately jabbed my elbow into her bony ribs. Subtlety was not one of my best friend's strong points. But luckily elbow jabbing was one of mine! (Lacey got the point and closed her trap.)

"I think she's great," Bethel enthused.

Huh? I blinked, dumbfounded. I was hardly expecting that! Maybe I wasn't expecting Bethel to dislike Ms. McGuire as strongly as I did, but thinking she was "great"? There was *no way* any human being in that classroom last week could have come away with that description . . . was there?

"I know she's not as soft or as sweet as Ms. Kern," Bethel continued, "but I have to say, I'm excited that we have someone no-nonsense around."

"Excited," I repeated dumbly, still amazed.

"You've got to admit, we need to get organized," Bethel insisted, training her big, dark eyes on mine. "And let's face it—Ms. McGuire is a lot more together in that department than Ms. Kern!"

"I wouldn't say that," I replied swiftly, jumping to Ms. Kern's defense. "Ms. Kern has done a lot for us," I added, annoyed that Bethel's memory seemed so short-term. I mean, Ms. Kern wasn't even *gone* yet!

"Hey." Bethel smiled confidently. "I'm not dissing Ms. Kern. I'm just pleased that Ms. McGuire is so focused. Maybe now we can get more done."

"Yeah," Lacey piped up sarcastically, ripping open a package of Twizzlers and peeling off a piece. "A little organization never hurts." Things like "being organized" and "getting things done" hardly registered on Lacey's list of things worth thinking about.

But I couldn't reply to Lacey or Bethel right now. I could only nod curtly and pull Lacey off to class while Bethel darted off down the hallway.

While we walked, Lacey blabbed away. She said something about "taking a chill pill"—input that I didn't exactly need to hear right now. So, Bethel didn't have a problem with Ms. McGuire, and I hadn't heard anyone else complaining. Either they were all out of the loop, or else the problem was mine.

Am I overreacting? I asked myself as Lacey and I took our seats. Was Ms. McGuire actually perfectly okay? Was *I* the one being a witch?

"Don't stress so much," Lacey said, patting me on the arm. She must have noticed that I was still feeling tense and mixed up. "You're a great president. Everyone thinks you're amazing. That's why you were voted in. So what's the big deal?"

But Lacey's words didn't do anything to cheer me up. In fact, they did the opposite. Instead of feeling confident, I started feeling more panicky. Maybe Lacey, and everyone else who voted for me, had overestimated my ability. Maybe I just wasn't president material.

I stared blankly at the white board and wished I knew the answer to even one of the questions going through my mind right then. But all I could really know for sure was that suddenly, nothing seemed simple.

Anna

Uh-oh! I thought as I watched Larissa heading down the hallway toward me. I thought about burying my head in my locker and trying to look anonymous, but I obviously wasn't going to fool anyone that way.

"Hey," I said with a weak smile, straightening up as she sashayed to a stop in front of me. As her face lit up in an expectant smile, I felt my spirits plummeting. I'd managed to avoid her call last night. But I couldn't avoid her forever.

"You, my girl, and *moi*, we need to have a serious yak about you know who," Larissa whispered excitedly, grabbing my arm and pulling me closer to the wall as a wave of students walked by. "Why didn't you call me back last night?" she demanded, bracelets jangling as she gripped my arm in anticipation.

"Sorry. I guess I just fell asleep," I lied.

"Sooo . . . what's the scoop? You must have managed to get *the* question out to him Saturday," she said, her eyes shining with excitement. "I left you guys alone for precisely that reason."

"I know," I said, unable to hide my unhappiness. I wished she *hadn't* left us alone. Because if Larissa and I had both been there on that park wall, then Toby would never have told me he liked me. And I'd never have had to ask him about Larissa. And all of us could just go back to being friends.

"I know you left me alone," I began as Larissa tapped her fingernails on the wall impatiently, showing no sign of giving up on her quest. "But I didn't get to ask him," I finished lamely.

Immediately I regretted the lie. Larissa's face fell. She went from being all elated to looking confused and disappointed. "Why not?" She frowned.

Now what? There was nothing I could say. I couldn't think of one good excuse for supposedly not finding out what Toby thought of Larissa. And now Larissa would just think I was the kind of friend who'd promise to help but couldn't get behind her words.

There was only one decent explanation for this whole thing, and as I looked at Larissa's furrowed brow and the confusion in her eyes, I knew I had no other choice. I was fresh out of choices, in fact.

The truth would have to do.

"Listen—," I began, but just then I was interrupted by the shrill, piercing sound of the school bell.

"Darn it," Larissa muttered, shrugging. "Talk later?" she asked, hoisting her book bag onto her shoulder. "I've got to fly," she added. "Keeping up my grades means getting to class on time. And unfortunately I have science, which is only, like, a hundred miles from here."

"Okay," I replied, and Larissa bounded off down the hallway.

I felt almost woozy from my near brush with disaster. Now at least I had bought a little more time to figure out how to put the truth to Larissa. Or maybe figure out something better than the truth.

"Hi, Anna." A perky voice interrupted my grim thoughts. I turned to see Elizabeth smiling at me, looking fresh and unfussed in pink capri pants. "Wow, Larissa should be on the track team," she added, laughing as we watched Larissa skidding around the corner of the hallway, her platform sneakers screeching as she braked and turned. "She almost knocked me off my feet," Elizabeth remarked, shaking her head with a smile.

"Oh, really?" I said absently.

"She's so great," Elizabeth chattered on. "You should send her the e-mail forward," she suggested.

"E-mail?" I looked up, trying to pick up on Elizabeth's train of thought and untangle myself from my own jumbled feelings.

"You know, the friendship-chain thing I sent you," Elizabeth answered as I went back to my locker and rummaged around for my copy of *Lord of the Flies,* which we were reading in English. "I mean, I hate chain letters and e-mail forwards and all that stuff," Elizabeth continued. "But I thought that one was really cute."

"Yeah," I replied, sighing inwardly as I remembered the words of Elizabeth's e-mail. *A true friend is hard to find. Don't take your friendship for granted.* Elizabeth was one of those kinds of friends. She'd probably be really understanding and supportive if I told her about the whole Toby situation. But now wasn't the time or the place, and besides, this was something I had to figure out on my own. I mean, look at what had happened when I told Salvador. It had only made me ten times more confused!

I smiled at Elizabeth, but my thoughts kept

turning back to Larissa. *Guess you're about to break the chain of friendship, Anna!* I thought miserably. Once Larissa knew the truth, she would hate me. And I wished more than ever that there was another way to get out of this. But there wasn't.

Toby

"Toby, you need to loosen up!" Mr. Dowd shouted from the back of the auditorium. "How are we supposed to believe that Tony loves Maria if he's holding her like she's an overgrown sardine?"

"Sorry," I mumbled, trying to relax my arms around Bianca's waist. Mr. Dowd was right. Tony had just made his great declaration of love to Maria, but there was no feeling there. I just couldn't get into character.

Maybe because I couldn't relate to Tony right now. The girl *he* liked totally liked him back. The girl *I* liked could barely stand to be alone with me.

I'd thought for sure that when I told Anna I liked her, I'd somehow hear her repeat the same words back to me. But apparently I was totally wrong. The weird vibes between us had had nothing to do with us liking each other. It had to do with me liking Anna and her *not* liking me!

"You have to show her your feelings," Mr.

Dowd lectured, breaking into my chain of thought.

Why? So she can reject me? No thanks! I thought bitterly, clenching my jaw. I looked over at Anna—who was sitting in one of the front rows, looking at her script. Today's play practice was just for the principal characters, so it was probably a lot easier to concentrate since it was a bit quieter than usual. But I could tell Anna wasn't really focusing on her script—she was obviously just trying to avoid any eye contact with me by hiding underneath her curtain of hair. (Apparently she couldn't even bear to look at me anymore!)

But then she looked up, and for just a fraction of an instant, our eyes met. Hers were totally expressionless, but her cheeks were burning. Obviously Mr. Dowd's speech had gotten to her.

She ducked away under her hair again, and I looked down at the floor, letting Mr. Dowd's stream of commands go right over my head. I couldn't concentrate on Mr. Dowd. Not right now, when I felt like such a total fool!

"Tony is a man of passion. He wears his heart on his sleeve," Mr. Dowd rambled on.

Well, he's an idiot! I thought as I nodded robotically at Mr. Dowd and smiled blankly at Bianca.

"But we're out of time," Mr. Dowd finished off. I exhaled with relief. Being up on that stage was so frustrating. I knew what I was supposed to be doing, but I just couldn't seem to do it. I'd had enough frustration for one week—I needed an intermission!

Still, as I saw Anna creeping toward the back of the auditorium, something in me kind of caved in. The awkwardness between us now was almost worse than the humiliation I felt. I mean, we'd been friends, and now we couldn't even look at each other!

I scowled and stared at the lines in my script without reading them. This whole thing was totally annoying. I should *never* have told Anna that I liked her!

But I couldn't change that now. *Lose the ego, Toby!* I ordered myself. *Get a grip!* The best I could do now was try and smooth things over between me and Anna so we could both forget this. Because we were going to have to rehearse together—that was something we couldn't change.

"Anna, wait up!" I shouted after her as she walked out through the back door of the theater.

I took a deep breath as I caught up with her, and she reluctantly turned to face me, her eyes still not meeting mine. "We have to talk," I started weakly, wishing I didn't have to do this. It was bad enough dealing with a bruised ego—facing the bruiser was no picnic either!

Toby

But there was no way around this one. And much as I wanted to let Anna walk away so I didn't have to deal, I also knew that I couldn't. We *did* have to talk. No matter how tough it was going to be. (And judging by the fact that she couldn't even look at me, "tough" seemed like the understatement of the year!)

Anna

"Look, I'm—I'm sorry about Saturday," Toby stammered, his hands jammed into his pockets as we stood facing each other on the steps outside the theater. "I guess I shouldn't have said anything. Me and my big mouth."

He smiled weakly. I looked away because it hurt me to see him struggling.

This is so hard! My stomach clenched while Toby went on. "It's okay that you don't like me back," he murmured, kicking at a loose stone on the steps. "I just want things to be cool between us. Like . . . friends." He looked up at me. "I mean, I hope we can be friends again."

"Okay." I stood there like a statue, my eyes on the stone steps. I couldn't walk away, but I didn't know what else to do. I just felt paralyzed, inside and out.

"So we're cool?" Toby spoke up softly.

"Yeah." I nodded and tried to smile.

"Okay . . . well . . ." Toby backed away and gave a little wave before turning around.

Anna

Wait! I wanted to shout, but the word wouldn't come out. I was such a mess. A well of panic sprang up in me as I watched Toby move away. The talk was over. And I hadn't said anything at all. Now he would go home feeling like I didn't like him. He deserved better than that!

"Toby," I called out. He stopped walking and turned around. "I have something to say."

Do you? the little voice inside my head questioned as my heart practically bashed a hole through my rib cage. Now that I had Toby's attention, I wasn't sure if I had the courage to do this. I took a deep breath.

"I-like-you-too-but-I-just-couldn't-say-so!" The words just burst out of me.

"You do?" Toby's smile was hesitant as he came back toward me. And as much as I tried, I couldn't stop myself from smiling back. There we were, two grinning idiots.

But then Toby's face clouded over in confusion. "So then, why . . . ?"

I shook my head to stop him from saying any more. "I can't tell you," I said, my heart heaving and my smile fading. "I still can't go out with you, but I can't say why."

I tried to swallow, but my mouth was as dry as sandpaper. All my feelings for Toby swirled around and mixed together with all the reasons why I couldn't do anything *about* those feelings. We could only be friends, no more than that. And I couldn't tell him why!

"Are you going out with someone else?" Toby queried, his eyebrows knitting together.

"No, it's nothing like that. It's . . ." I bit my lip and trailed off. "I'm sorry, but I can't say any more. It wouldn't be fair."

"To who?" Toby prodded, but I just shook my head. I didn't want to betray Larissa. It would be hard enough for her to hear that Toby didn't like her—I mean, I knew I'd have to tell her that. But the least I could do was help her save face by not directly telling Toby that she liked him.

"Are you saying that if you went out with me, it would be unfair to someone else?" Toby quizzed. I nodded, keeping my lips zipped.

"Is that someone else maybe, like, Larissa or something?" he added after a moment of silence.

Uh-oh! I sucked in some air and clamped my jaw, wondering wildly what I'd said to make him guess. And then I realized. *Duh!* I mean, it was *obvious!* I'd asked him if he liked her Saturday, and I'd spent all of last week trying to talk to him about Larissa and how great she was!

But somehow I guess I didn't think he'd figure it out. Guys can be dumb about that stuff, and maybe if someone less clued in were standing in front of me right then, they wouldn't have had the faintest idea what was going on.

No chance of that, though. Toby was too smart and sensitive to be duped.

"It is Larissa, isn't it?"

I sighed and sat down on the steps. In a way, I was relieved to finally have the truth out there so I didn't have to keep everything hidden away anymore. But that didn't make the situation any easier.

"She's my friend," I explained to Toby. "*Our* friend," I corrected myself. "It just wouldn't be right for you and me to go out."

"So that's why you've been acting so strangely." Toby sat down next to me. "All the questions about Larissa. Now I get it."

"Yep." I nodded, a bleak smile on my face. Everything was out in the open now. In a movie that would mean a happy ending. Unfortunately this was my life! And what should have been a high point was actually a total mess.

"But if you like me and I like you, we should be able to work things out, right?" Toby looked searchingly at me. "There's nothing wrong with liking each other. I mean, we're not doing it to hurt Larissa."

"That doesn't make a difference," I shot back, folding my arms. "It would hurt her no matter what. And I don't want to go out with you if it ends up hurting a friend."

Because I know what it feels like! I wanted to say, but I didn't. I didn't need to tell Toby about Elizabeth and Salvador. The important thing was that *I* knew about it. And although Larissa would find out soon enough that Toby didn't like her except as a friend, the least I could do was spare her from seeing us as a couple.

"I understand . . . I guess." Toby tried to shoot me his trademark lopsided grin, but I could see he felt disappointed. "You're a good friend to Larissa, and that's really good. I like that about you."

"Thanks." I stood up awkwardly and slung my backpack over my shoulder. "Well, I guess I'll see you tomorrow."

"Yeah." Toby's eyes met mine, and I could see he wanted to say more but thought better of it. "Guess I better hit the road," he added, jerking his head in the direction of his bicycle.

"Bye."

For a moment I pictured how this scene could have played out if Larissa hadn't liked Toby. Maybe right now Toby and I would be on our way to I Scream for sundaes. Or maybe making plans to see each other after school tomorrow.

But I guess it just wasn't meant to be. And as

Toby turned and walked toward the bike rack, his shoulders slumped, I felt a sad emptiness in the pit of my stomach. I knew I'd done the right thing, and now Toby, Larissa, and I could all go back to being friends, but still!

I guess being right doesn't always make you *feel* right.

"Thanks, Mom," I murmured as I slammed the door to my mom's car. I'd asked her to drop me off at Salvador's house because I needed to do some homework stuff with him, which was partly true. But mostly I just didn't want to go home and be alone in my room with all my jumbled thoughts and feelings.

"Sal?" I called out as I opened the front door.

"Hello, Anna, *querida!*" the Doña greeted me, coming to the door in an apron. "He's not home yet. Band practice, I think. But come in, come in!" The Doña patted my back and steered me into the kitchen.

"I'm baking an apple cake," she announced, pointing at the oven.

"Smells great," I said, with a tired smile. And it did—the whole house smelled of cinnamon and apples. But I wasn't hungry. "Did he say when he'd be back?" I asked the Doña. I was anxious to see Salvador. I mean, he was the only person who really knew about my problem, and I needed his advice before I went and spoke to Larissa.

"Soon," the Doña reassured me, pouring me a glass of homemade lemonade. "You look like you need a little refreshment," she added, eyeing me closely. I sighed and nodded. *I need more than that,* I thought grimly, climbing onto a stool.

I was completely confused over what I should say to Larissa. There was no point in telling her about Toby liking me. That would only make her feel even more wounded. And since I'd told Toby we couldn't go out, I could keep that little detail a secret. Still, I wasn't sure how to break the rest of it, how to actually tell Larissa that Toby didn't want to go out with her.

"So . . . did your friend Hannah sort things out with that boy she liked?" the Doña asked, removing the cake from the oven.

Is the Doña reading my mind? I thought. "Not really," I murmured glumly, staring dismally into my glass of lemonade. "It's still a big mess."

"Did she ever find out if the boy liked her too?" the Doña pressed.

"Yeah, and he does," I replied with a sigh. "But that only makes things worse. She doesn't want to hurt Larissa—her friend," I explained.

"I see." The Doña was silent as she slid the

cake from the pan. But I could tell she had something on her mind.

"What do you think she should do?" I asked, anxious to hear what the Doña was thinking. "I mean, she has no choice," I continued. "She *has* to lie! It's a white lie, though . . . right?"

The Doña was silent for a few more seconds, and then she stared at me with her bright black eyes. "A lie never does anyone any good," she murmured kindly. "Once a lie is discovered, it always make things worse."

"But what if the truth is really painful?" I blurted out, my voice heavy with emotion. "A lie can't be worse than that!"

I bit my lip and tried to compose myself. After all, this was supposed to be "Hannah's" problem, not mine.

"Sooner or later, lies always catch up to you," the Doña responded, nodding thoughtfully while she started to cut the cake. "And this Larissa, she deserves to have the truth."

"But maybe if Hannah just stays out of the picture, then Toby *would* like Larissa," I suggested. "They get along really well anyway. It's just Hannah that's standing in the way!" Tears burned at the back of my throat, but I gulped them down. Crying wasn't going to help me here. I *had* to keep it together!

"Why force someone to like someone they do not have feelings for?" the Doña asked, pausing to fix me with her shrewd gaze. "If two people like each other, is it fair to try and make one of them like someone else? No!" she said emphatically. "It's not fair to *anyone!*"

I heaved another sigh and tried to hold things together. The Doña was right. And suddenly the old situation with Elizabeth and Salvador and me suddenly swam into focus.

For the first time I realized that *everyone* had gotten hurt because we were all trying to force something that wasn't really happening. I'd tried to make Salvador like me when he didn't. And he'd tried to get Elizabeth to be his girlfriend when she wasn't ready. And everyone was lying to each other.

"Thank you, Doña," I murmured, almost to myself, as I slipped off the stool and picked up my backpack. Listening to someone as wise as the Doña had really paid off. I didn't need to wait for Salvador anymore.

"Leaving so soon?" the Doña asked. I wasn't sure, but I thought I detected a suspicious tone in her voice.

"Oh yeah . . . I realized I have someone I need to talk to," I responded.

"Are you sure you don't want to wait till the apple cake is ready?"

"Yes, I'm sure, but thank you for asking." By that time I was already halfway out the door.

"I wish Hannah the best of luck," she added. "I hope she does the right thing. But knowing her, I think she will."

I threw her a confused backward glance as I headed out onto the patio. She didn't *know* Hannah. At least, she didn't *know* she knew Hannah.

As the screen door slammed shut, the Doña just threw me a wink and went back to cutting the cake.

Kristin

"Thank you, everyone!" Ms. Kern called out, raising her cup of punch. "I'm going to miss you all," she added, her eyes moistening with tears.

I raised my cup of punch to her along with everyone else. She caught my eye and mouthed "thank you" to me, which made me glow with pride.

I'd spent loads of time over the past few days, helping to organize Ms. Kern's going-away party. It was I who'd done the big flower arrangement of lilies and ferns in the center of the gym, and I'd also organized the catering and gotten the silver, sparkly balloons with Good-bye, Ms. K. lettered on them.

Considering all the negative feelings I'd been having lately about my own self-worth, it was nice to feel just a little bit proud of this. I could do *something* right, it seemed, even if I wasn't a good student-government president.

"Hi, Kristin." I turned to find Ms. McGuire

standing behind me. She was wearing a smart, narrow, green pantsuit, and her makeup was immaculate as always. Me, on the other hand . . . well, I knew I looked a wreck. I'd spent half the morning blowing up balloons, and I probably looked like a chipmunk by now! A chipmunk in a wrinkled skirt. I saw the way Ms. McGuire's eyes flitted over me. . . . Apparently she'd noticed.

"Kristin, I thought we were going to get together for a one-on-one last week," she said in a slightly cool tone. "Weren't you going to check in with me so we could schedule that?"

"I'm . . . sorry," I murmured, hating myself for blushing. "I guess I've just been so caught up in organizing the party and everything," I explained hastily.

"I see," Ms. McGuire replied evenly, and shot me one of her brief insta-smiles. "Well, maybe we can do it later this week?"

"Yes, of course. I'll, um, consult my schedule and get back to you."

Way to go, Kristin! I berated myself as Ms. McGuire walked off to join the other teachers. Much as I wanted to, this time I couldn't blame Ms. McGuire for being slightly clipped with me. After all, I *had* said I'd get back to her, and I didn't. I was the flake, and she was right to call me on it.

Great, now she has even more ammunition to back up her opinion of me. An opinion that was probably already rock-bottom low. *And maybe she's right!* I thought miserably, chipping away at my polystyrene punch cup with my fingernail. *Why should Ms. McGuire think I'm any good at my job when I'm not exactly behaving like a reliable student president!*

I should just resign! A lump formed in my throat as I crushed my empty punch cup and tossed it into the garbage. That seemed to be my only option. It would probably be the right thing to do for the sake of the student government. That way Bethel or someone else who had a better relationship with Ms. McGuire could take over, and everyone would be better off.

"Kristin!" I tried to smile and look cheerful as Ms. Kern came toward me, her face lighting up. "What a lovely party you've put on for me!"

I thanked her and tried to look cheerful as she exclaimed over the food, the flowers, and the decor, but inside I felt as shriveled and deflated as one of the dying helium balloons falling from the gym ceiling.

"You know, you have a real gift," Ms. Kern

continued, squeezing my shoulder. "Everything you set your mind to, you pull off."

"Thank you," I replied, touched by Ms. Kern's compliment even though I didn't really believe it. I mean, I'd dropped the ball—big time—with Ms. McGuire. All week long I'd been freaked out, incoherent, and totally disorganized—hardly the way to rack up points in the good-leadership-skills department.

"I'm serious, you know," Ms. Kern continued, putting both hands on my shoulders so I was forced to look her in the eye. "I also know you doubt yourself sometimes," she murmured. I could only nod. Ms. Kern knows me really well. Putting on an act for her would never work.

"I guess I just feel . . . overwhelmed," I admitted with a pained smile.

"Well, you have an overwhelming job!" Ms. Kern replied sympathetically. "But Kristin, you are a natural-born leader. I knew it from the moment I met you. And I have tremendous faith in your capabilities."

"Really?" *Natural-born leader?* I'm not saying I believed Ms. Kern's words, but they definitely made me feel better. Suddenly I felt kind of light—almost happy.

"Absolutely!" Ms. Kern nodded vigorously.

"This is a tough time for you, but I have no doubt in my mind that you will do a wonderful job without me. The students are extremely lucky to have you."

"I'm not so sure about that!" I coughed a little and tried to smile, but it was hard. I still had so many doubts about the job ahead of me, about Ms. McGuire—and of course, doubts about myself.

"Kristin, listen to me. No one can do this better than you! If anyone could, they would have been voted in. But they weren't because you're the girl for the job." Ms. Kern gave my shoulders another tight squeeze and then grinned. "So go get 'em!"

Wow, she really believes in me! I thought, feeling something inside me loosen up and relax, as if a rubber band that had been wound around my insides had suddenly snapped. I shouldn't have been surprised by Ms. Kern's pep talk—I mean, of course I knew she was on my side. But I guess I'd been so focused on all the negatives that somehow I'd lost sight of what my strengths were.

And it did mean something—after all, Ms. Kern was a teacher, and if she had confidence in me, then there must be a reason for it.

"Okay, I'll do my best," I said to Ms. Kern,

and felt my face twitch into the first real smile I'd had on my face in days! And at that moment everything I'd been dragging with me just kind of melted away. *I* can *do this!* I thought excitedly. And I knew I would. With or without Ms. McGuire's help I would lead the student body, and I would give it my all!

"You look like Kristin Seltzer," a voice piped up as Ms. Kern moved off to speak to some of the other students. "The Kristin Seltzer I know!"

"Brian!" I swatted my hand at his arm, still grinning. "That's correct—Kristin Seltzer is back in the house."

"Good, because I've missed you." Relief flickered in Brian's light green eyes. "It's good to see you smiling."

"Well, I think some unhappy impostor took over my body, but she just left the building." I grinned and accepted another cup of punch from Brian. Right then I really did feel like I was "back." Like I'd just taken a yoga class or gone for a long swim in a mountain lake and was now totally relaxed. And back to my old self.

Brian tugged at a loose curl that had sprung out from under my headband, and I rolled my eyes, feeling like everything was where it should be. Student government didn't have to be a war zone. Not if I approached it right.

So I vowed right then and there that the real Kristin would stay. She wouldn't be intimidated or frazzled by anyone.

Least of all Ms. McGuire!

Anna

"Larissa's upstairs!" Mrs. Harris trilled in her British accent as she let me into the Harris home. "You know where to find her!"

I climbed each step of the spiral staircase with mounting dread. *Easy does it,* I told myself as the panicked knot in my stomach began to grow. But with every step I could hear the words *traitor* and *backstabber* shooting through me like arrows. It didn't matter how much I reasoned this out—I still felt awful.

"You're here!" Larissa yelped, springing out from her bedroom in Chinese pajamas. "Seven fifty-nine P.M.," she added, consulting her Hello Kitty watch. "You're a minute early! *Excellent!*"

Boy, was this going to be hard! I followed Larissa into her bedroom and climbed the ladder to her loft bed. She looked so excited and bouncy and happy. I couldn't believe that I had to be the bearer of bad news. *I* was going to be the downer, the one who turned her from majorly happy to majorly miserable. Me!

But I couldn't think like that. I had a purpose, and I knew I had to stick by my decision—to tell the truth. The whole truth and nothing but.

"So do you have any news for me?" Larissa grilled me as we sat on the bed, facing each other.

I swallowed and gripped the pillow in my lap for support. "Yes, I do," I said quietly. "I'm really sorry, Larissa, but the truth is going to hurt."

"What do you mean?" Suddenly the spark was gone from Larissa's eyes, and she looked at me warily. "Just tell me, Anna. What's up? You have such a weird look on your face." We sat in silence for a few seconds.

"I like Toby." I finally blurted it out. Just like that. But I could barely hear my own words above the hammering of my heart. "I've liked him for a while. And I think he likes me too," I added, wincing as I saw Larissa's expression transform from excitement into disbelief. "I've just been too scared to tell you."

"Is this some kind of joke?" Larissa stared at me with wide, disbelieving eyes. "Because it's not funny."

"No, it's not," I said in a low voice, tears prickling at my eyelids. There was no going back now. Larissa was going to hate my guts after this. But I had to get through it and tell her everything. It was the least I could do—for both of us.

"When you say you *think* he likes you too, you mean you *know* he does," Larissa said slowly and coldly. "Am I right?"

I nodded and then stared into my lap. I couldn't bear to see the tears glittering in Larissa's eyes or the hurt look that I knew covered every inch of her formerly happy face.

"How could you do this to me?" Larissa shouted suddenly, and I looked up to see a tear drop onto her cheek and roll down to her chin. "You *knew* I liked him!"

"Yes, I knew," I tried to explain, the words spilling out of me as I rushed to defend myself and our friendship. "That's why I kept my feelings to myself. I didn't want to hurt you, so I didn't tell Toby how I felt. I didn't say one word. Except what you wanted me to say!"

"So are you two going out now—behind my back?" Larissa asked coldly, angrily brushing away her tears.

"No!" I replied in a pleading tone. I grabbed for her hand, but she snatched it away. All I could do was explain to her my side of the story. And I did. I told her how bad I'd felt, how much I'd tried *not* to like Toby, how many nights I'd tossed and turned over this.

And even though she spent the whole time

staring at me like she was made of stone, she did at least listen to me. Especially when I told her how much I'd feared this scene because of what had happened to me with Elizabeth and Salvador.

"I know how this feels. Believe me," I said finally. "That's why I tried to stop myself from liking him. And that's why I acted as the go-between between you and Toby. Because friendship comes first."

Right then, I was surprised to see a slight softening in Larissa's face. I wouldn't say she looked sympathetic exactly, but she did look less like she wanted to kill me. "Well, I have to say, I never would have guessed this," she began slowly. "I mean, you definitely kept your feelings hidden, all right."

"I guess I hoped they'd just disappear. Or at least fade once you and Toby got together," I said feebly.

Was I imagining things, or was there a fraction of a smile on Larissa's face? For a moment hope flickered through me, but just as quickly, it snuffed itself out. Who was I kidding? Larissa would never forgive me for this, even if she knew I hadn't tried to hurt her deliberately.

"Lying to yourself, helping me with my Toby q-and-a mission . . . you did all that for me?" she asked, her voice quavering. "Wow," she said, sniffling. "I have to say, Anna, that's pretty amazing of you."

"Really?" My heart leaped, and I searched her face for more of a sign that she might actually forgive me . . . but I couldn't quite tell where she was with all this. Obviously she was still processing everything, and she needed her space. Out of respect I decided not to push it—I just closed my mouth and sat there. I mean, even if Larissa wanted to use me as a punching bag right now, I would understand—I *had* lied to her for weeks.

"I can't say I feel great right now," Larissa continued quietly, balling a Kleenex in her fist, "but I'd be a liar if I said I didn't admire you for what you did." She looked up at me then, really looked at me. But not in a mean way. "I can't believe what a good friend you've been," she continued. "Putting yourself through all of this for me."

"Well, you're my friend," I broke in, wiping at my own eyes with my fingers.

"You're right about that," Larissa replied, and then she *did* smile. Really smile. "You know I'd love to say I'd have done the same thing if I had been in your shoes, but I don't know if I'd have had the strength. I mean, I positively adore you, but giving up Toby? I'm not sure I could have!"

And right then, maybe for no reason at all, we burst out laughing. And then the greatest thing happened. Larissa leaned over and gave me a hug.

"I'm happy for you," she added as we broke apart. "Really, you should go for Toby. You deserve him. You're loyal and cool, and he deserves that too."

"But what about you?" I said quietly. Larissa was putting on a brave face, but I could tell she was still pretty upset.

"Hey, with trying to keep my grades up *and* the play, I don't really have time for a boyfriend," Larissa said, hugging her knees to her chest and struggling to grin.

"What about having a date for opening night?" I asked.

"Oh, a date would just end up getting in between me and my public," she replied, and blew her nose loudly.

That's Larissa for you.

"Really, Anna, I'll be fine," she added.

"Okay," I replied, taking her hand. This time she let me. The smile on her face made me feel like a concrete brick had been lifted off my shoulders.

I still had a friend, and I still had a chance with Toby. The Doña had been right all along—the truth does set you free!

* * *

Anna

"Those dancers are going to *make* this show," Toby said as we watched the opening dance sequence onstage. Jets and Sharks alike, everyone was nailing the dance that Ms. Hudson had choreographed, including Larissa. But I couldn't focus on that because I kept stealing sideways glances at Toby.

Even though Toby seemed happy to talk to me and gave a running commentary throughout the performance, I knew it was an effort for him. He still wasn't quite back to his natural self around me, and he was keeping his eyes very firmly on the stage.

I swallowed, wondering if there was some way, some signal I could give him to let him know that I'd had a change of heart—well, maybe not a change of heart exactly, since I'd always known where my heart had been . . . but a change of plan.

But changing my plans was one thing and telling Toby about it, well, that was trickier. I'm not the kind of person who would just jump up and say, "Let's go out with each other!" And since I hadn't told Toby about my talk with Larissa, I couldn't exactly clue him in as to how I was feeling right now.

Except maybe in some sort of code.

"You know," I began slowly, "if we did a

rewrite of this play, I'd like to see Tony and Anita end up together."

Toby was silent for a moment. I almost didn't think he'd heard me, but then he turned to face me, for the first time giving me a full frontal instead of the profile. "Tony and Anita, huh?" he asked, looking me over as if he was trying to guess my meaning. "Well, that's a . . . big rewrite."

"Rewrites are possible," I murmured, feeling a flush spring to my cheeks. "Sometimes they make the ending better."

"But Anita wouldn't go out with Tony," Toby replied evenly. "Because she'd be betraying her friend if she did." The lights were low in the auditorium, but I could still make out the questioning look in his eyes.

"Not in my version," I retorted as we watched the dancers spin and leap. "In my version the friend tells her it's okay."

"Hmmm. I like that version," Toby joked, and I smiled to myself as we went back to watching the dancers. And that was that. No further explanation required. That's another bonus in the endless series of things that are great about Toby—he totally gets me.

The truth had worked out—well, maybe not the entire truth. I'd decided not to tell Larissa that Toby *had* figured out she liked him. But I didn't see that as a lie, and I'm sure even the Doña would agree with me.

And I knew Larissa would be back to her normal, perky self in no time. She was up there on the stage right now, having a blast. She even waved at me and Toby at one point, and we waved back. She's just one of those people who doesn't let setbacks bother her too much.

I sat back in the plush auditorium seat and felt myself relax completely for the first time in forever! My hands slipped down at my sides, and I closed my eyes, trying to picture how things would end in this drama.

But there's always a twist to every story, I guess. And I was surprised by the one that came next. As I lay back, I suddenly felt something—some*one*—touch my hand. The hand was a little bigger than mine. And as it closed around my own, between the seats where no one could see, I felt like a thousand little fireworks were exploding in my heart.

I stared ahead, and Toby stared ahead, watching the dancers. My hand in his.

It was the best feeling in the world.

Francine Pascal's
SWEET VALLEY
jr. high